Coming of Age
13 B'NAI MITZVAH
STORIES

edited by Jonathan Rosen and Henry Herz

Albert Whitman & Company
Chicago, Illinois

With thanks to all the parents, other family members, and teachers who help young people prepare for accepting the burden of responsible adulthood and striving to make the world a better place—JR and HH

Library of Congress Cataloging-in-Publication data is on file with the publisher.

First published in the United States of America in 2022
by Albert Whitman & Company
ISBN 978-0-8075-3667-4 (hardcover)
ISBN 978-0-8075-3666-7 (ebook)

Printed in the United States of America
10 9 8 7 6 5 4 3 2 1 LB 26 25 24 23 22 21

Jacket art by Ilana Griffo
Design by Rick DeMonico

For more information about Albert Whitman & Company, visit our website at www.albertwhitman.com.

Contents

Introduction

Reading helps build bridges.

It gives us an entry point into other worlds, communities, and beliefs. Perhaps, by gaining a little more understanding, better relations will happen.

Over the last eight years, the number of anti-Semitic attacks in the United States has steadily risen. Jews make up less than three percent of the population, yet statistically, the highest percentage of hate crimes are perpetuated against them. In Europe, the numbers are even larger. Attacks on Jews and Jewish institutions have become an all-too-common occurrence across the US. There has also been an increase in Holocaust denial, with more than half of Americans not knowing fully what happened to Europe's Jewish population during World War II. In a 2020 study commissioned by the Conference on Jewish Material Claims Against Germany, it was revealed that two-thirds of Americans didn't know what Auschwitz was.

While this book isn't going to cure anti-Semitism—even though a portion of the proceeds is going to go to organizations that will help fight it—what this book *will* do is bring some fun Jewish stories into your hands. The hands of readers. Not only is it important for Jewish kids to be able to see themselves and their experiences in books, but it's also good to have non-Jewish kids see that Jewish kids aren't so different from them after all. As I said, reading helps build bridges. So maybe, just maybe, it can all start with a book.

Most likely, you or someone you love bought you this book because you're at that age. The age of B'nai Mitzvah. Well, just like Jews across the world, the B'nai Mitzvah stories in this anthology are an eclectic bunch. Some are pure fiction; some are based on fact. Some are more serious, and some are on the funnier side, proving that there is no one right way to celebrate. However you do it is the right way for you. But whatever it is you do, please enjoy it, remember it, and take notes. It is your B'nai Mitzvah, a ritual passed down from many a generation before you, and hopefully, for many more after. And perhaps one day, you'll write your own story for a future generation of kids going through their own Bar or Bat Mitzvah.

Until then, thank you for reading. We wish you mazel tov and hope you enjoy this collection of stories!

Jonathan Rosen

Ceremony

Jane Yolen

Whether or not there is a ceremony,
you will come of age.
Life hands you days, years,
not parties.
It is the days that count,
the years.
"Wear them well,"
my grandmother used to say.
And I do,
even though Bat Mitzvahs
hadn't been invented yet.

The Assignment

Sarah Aronson

The week Richard Nixon resigned as president, the rabbi called my mom and me into his office to give me my assigned Torah portion for my upcoming Bat Mitzvah. Altogether, he gave me three copies of some Hebrew phrases, plus translation and transliteration—in case my Hebrew was lacking.

It didn't seem like enough.

This was supposed to be my big day, the day I became a Jewish adult. I looked at the title of my parashah. "Kedoshim?" My heart sank. "Isn't that one of the laws chapters?"

(I had been hoping for something juicy from Exodus.)

Maybe he'd seen this disappointment before, because without sighing or clearing his throat or reaching for one of his heavy books about Judaism, he said, "Sarah." (Full stop.) "Next April, you're going to become the third Bat Mitzvah in this congregation." (Another full stop.) "I thought you'd be excited to tackle a parashah as hefty as this one." (Now a smile at my mom.) "It will give you a chance to say everything you want to say."

I had a whole lot to say—that was no secret.

He continued to sell it. "Kedoshim is part of the holiness code. You're going to find it very inspiring." He took a very long, very slow breath. "Especially when it comes to women."

Now I perked up.

"For example," he told us, "in the Ten Commandments, it says honor your father and mother, but the Torah uses the word, *revere*. It also puts the woman first."

I slumped down in my chair. Rabbis! They were so obsessed with technicalities! This was not the feminist breakthrough I had dreamed of. I wanted to talk about revolution—not syntax.

Before I could protest, Mom squeezed my hand hard. I knew what that meant.

She didn't want me to embarrass her. Or make a stink. Or be rude to the rabbi.

For her, I said, "Thank you." As they continued to talk, I thought about everything I'd learned in the last two years. Maybe the rabbi had a point. There *were* a lot of laws that needed to be changed.

Thanks to a Fulbright scholarship, my family had spent much of the previous year living in York, England, a city with a giant cathedral and a wall. That year, while my friends at home worried about band tryouts, boys, grades, and Watergate, we visited museums, walked the moors, and stood by while friends took the O Levels—a countrywide test. It was a time of fun and discovery. We hid American pennies everywhere we went: behind the sign at the bed-and-breakfast, in a crack at Fountains Abbey, on the stairs of the great York Minster. The whole time, we looked at home from a distance.

This changed how I saw the world. And justice. And fairness. Returning home had only made it harder.

The truth was, since returning home, I'd found my hometown of Bethlehem, Pennsylvania, both stifling and frustrating. It wasn't just that I missed the adventure of living in England. Or even eating fish and chips out of newspaper. In a town called Bethlehem, it was not easy being Jewish.

> Aug 9, 1974
>
> Dear Diary,
>
> Nixon resigned! Isn't that the best news ever?
>
> Unfortunately, Tommy didn't want to celebrate. In fact, the only reason he came over was to tell me that when school started up, he was not going to carry my trumpet. Why was this happening? Well, it was because I am Jewish. You see, Diary, Tommy is Catholic. And his mother told him that I was going to go to a terrible place (or in her words, H E Double Toothpicks) and thus, he should stay away from me as much as absolutely possible. (Side note: If you recall, he also knows that there is no Santa because of me, and I am

pretty sure his mom still hates me for that.)

Yours,

Sarah

For the record, this was not my first confrontation with anti-Semitism. (It wouldn't be my last either.) Also, I didn't like playing the trumpet! I had wanted to play a lighter instrument—like the clarinet—but the dentist feared it would make my overbite worse. Trumpet, he insisted, would push those teeth back in—I wouldn't need braces. He was right. It also meant I was the only girl in my section. Only girl. Only Jew. I needed some backup.

That's why, just before Presidents' Day vacation, when my teacher gave us a biography assignment, I thought that this could be my chance to write about someone who looked and sounded like me—a Jewish woman—and at the same time, get a head start on my Bat Mitzvah speech—I still hadn't written a word.

But when I looked down the list of Recommended Subjects, all I felt was disappointment.

There were the usual suspects: George Washington, Abraham Lincoln, Jesus (yes, Jesus), and Ted Kennedy. Jim Thorpe was a favorite back then, as was Joe Namath.

But no Jews.

Or women.

I was about to mount a very loud and angry protest, when I saw a name added in pencil to the bottom of the list. It was a name I didn't recognize: Abbie Hoffman.

I had no idea who she was, but Abbie was a girl's name and Hoffman sounded pretty Jewish to me. I circled her name and walked home with Tommy, who still wouldn't carry my trumpet, but my backpack was on his shoulder, and he had stopped talking about hell, which had become a fair enough compromise.

> Feb 15, 1975
>
> Dear Diary,
>
> After school, Tommy walked me home. He is soooooooooo cute. When we stopped at the mailbox, he reached over and kissed me, but only for a second. He told me he has forgiven me for the whole Santa thing.
>
> Yours,
>
> Sarah

That day, by the time I got home, all I could think about were lips. And kissing. And the mailbox. I forgot all about Abigail Hoffman until a month later, the night before my paper was due, when Tommy called me to find out if I was done. With two hours before lights out, I opened my *World Book Encyclopedia*. Volume H.

Abbie was not there.

I was not deterred. In Bethlehem, Pennsylvania, *Recommended Subjects* had to be encyclopedia worthy, so I crossed the hall to my sister's room, where Mom kept the Britannicas. These large blue books were not my favorite, because the print was smaller and the volumes were fatter.

Still, no Abigail Hoffman. Or even A. Hoffman. Or for that

matter, any Hoffman at all. It didn't make sense. So I looked under *A*. And then I tried *W* for women. And when I was all out of ideas, I made up an excuse for not doing this earlier.

(I was good at that.)

This was also not the first time I'd flubbed an assignment. So I knew what I had to do. I walked downstairs to suck it up and ask my parents for help.

They were sitting on the couch listening to the Beatles.

I said, "I have to write a paper about Abigail Hoffman, and she is not in either encyclopedia."

I tried to sound very indignant.

"Do you mean Abbie Hoffman?" my dad asked.

Mom's face turned red. She downed the rest of whatever she was drinking and turned off the music.

"Yes. Abigail Hoffman." I thought, *Grown-ups were so weird.*

My father said nothing as my mother, with a noticeable spring in her step, left the room, only to come back with an old shoebox covered in duct tape. "His name is Abbie Hoffman. He was the leader of the Chicago Eight—or Seven, depending on what book you're reading. He was part of this group called the Yippees. He was also my date to a prom."

"So he's not a woman?"

My father seemed annoyed. "Why are you writing about him? The guy never met a podium he didn't like. Isn't he in jail? I beat him in tennis four years in a row."

During the next hour, I listened to stories about Abbot (Abbie) Hoffman. I learned that he was a political activist, one of the demonstrators at the Democratic National Convention. I learned that he used humor to incite anger, that his protests were full of theater and a desire for justice. I even heard about his Bar Mitzvah (officiated by my grandpa), as well as the nights they went out and the four times he came back to Clark from Brandeis to battle my father across the net. Although my mother swore he was the most annoying boy in her class, they had kept in touch after college. Even better, there were more than a few pictures of the two of them together, and in all of them, my mom was smiling.

Abbie Hoffman grew up in Worcester, Massachusetts, and his family belonged to the congregation my grandfather served as head rabbi. I was more than secretly delighted to open one of his books to read his scathing memories of my grandfather's Jewish politics as well as the tiny mention of a girl.

My mother.

A girl who hadn't had the chance to read from the Torah.

As I wrote my paper, I thought about those rules and my Bat Mitzvah. I was going to break this glass ceiling for myself and for her.

March 20, 1975

Dear Diary,

All I can say is WOW. My mom kissed Abbie Hoffman. I am sure of it! There is a picture of her in a dress that was definitely not on a sale rack. And her hair was LONG. And she was smiling.

I am SO going to get an A on this paper.

Yours,

Sarah

I did get an A, the only one of that year. I also read Abbie's books as well as the books that were important to him. Reading about this rebel and imagining my mom as a girl gave me even more to think about, especially what it meant to be a Jewish woman. In those black on white words, I saw permission to speak up for what I thought was important. To do things my way.

In more than one way.

A few weeks before my Bat Mitzvah, my mom asked the rabbi for permission for me to narrate my uncle's jazz cantata as part of my ceremony—and he said yes. (Only one person was offended!) We baked cookies and stored them in freezers all over the neighborhood. I invited my school friends to come.

I finished my speech.

I thought about what *reverence* meant. In terms of women. In terms of ideas. And protest. I thought about what I wanted to contribute to my future. I thought a lot about Abbie.

Abbie taught me to trust my gut. And be skeptical. And state my opinions. Later, when I actually met him, he told me to work for what I wanted—even when it seemed unattainable. Long before I ever thought I would become a writer, he urged me to find my voice. To do something that mattered.

To change the world.

But it was my mom that showed me *how* I could do all that. She gave me permission to make mistakes. To choose my own battles. And express myself the way I wanted to be seen. She showed me that the world was changing. She showed me how she, and other women like her, had paved the way for our generation to do more. She showed me that I would pave the way too. Progress for women would happen.

(And look! We're getting there!)

April 25, 1975

Dear Diary,

I just got through my Bat Mitzvah! It was great! The cantata was amazing—all the rabbis said that that was the first time they'd seen drums on the bimah.

The cookies were good too.

I got $1000, a heart necklace from Tommy, and a huge stack of Jewish books. Mom says they will look good in my office someday. Although I am not sure if I am the kind of person who will ever have an office, I am saving them on the top shelf. They are sooooooooo heavy.

Yours,

Sarah (the newest official Jewish adult)

Snowball

Nora Raleigh Baskin

Hiding in the bathroom at the Hyatt Regency in Stamford, Connecticut, was not where Annie expected to be tonight, or *ever* for that matter, even if it was the nicest bathroom she had ever seen in her life. She didn't have to stand on the toilet to keep her feet from being visible under the door and risk anybody finding her. There was a full, solid wooden door that shut and locked.

There was enough space for a small table with a box of tissues and a miniature vase of flowers on top. The floor was a shiny, white marble like a perfectly smooth ice-skating rink.

It was like a whole little room unto itself in here.

Best of all, it was quiet.

Until Annie heard the bathroom door open, letting in a whoosh of thumping music from down the hall. Then soft footsteps entering the bathroom and an urgent knocking.

"Annie? Are you in there?"

"Is that you, Caroline?"

"Yes, it's me. Let me in."

Annie pushed open the swinging door. "Come, come. Hurry, hurry."

Once her friend was inside, Annie shut the stall door again. She clicked the latch back into place.

"Wow, it's huge in here," Caroline said, looking around.

"I know. Right?" Annie sat back down on the lid of the toilet.

Caroline stepped on the pedal of the tiny trash bin on the floor next to the little table with the flowers on top. It opened the lid. It banged shut.

"Shhh." Annie put her finger to her lips.

"Why did you leave me out there?" Caroline whispered.

"I didn't," Annie said, even though of course she had. Caroline was Annie's best friend, but even a best friend couldn't help with this problem. Still, Annie shouldn't have run away without telling Caroline where she was.

"How long have you been in here?" Caroline asked.

How long?

Since the music started for sure. Maybe before that?

No, just after, she told Caroline.

"Well, that explains a lot."

"Explains a lot *what*?"

"I've been looking—"

"Wait, someone's coming in," Annie interrupted.

The thumping vibrations of the music and the DJ's voice thundered in again when the door to the bathroom was pushed open. Chattering voices and clicking heels echoed, coming to a stop in front of the sink. Annie and Caroline froze. And listened. Because, well, that's what you do when you're hiding in the toilet stall at the Hyatt Regency in Stamford, Connecticut.

"Your mother let you wear lipstick?"

"It's gloss."

"Well, it looks like lipstick."

"It's gloss."

"Fine, it's gloss. Whatever. I was going to tell you it looked pretty but now never mind."

"Do I? Do you think I look pretty?"

Caroline widened her eyes as far as she could get them to widen, and she mouthed to Annie: *O-M-G, it's Sasha Binder.*

Annie shook her head the tiniest bit and tried to give her best what-do-I-care look with a slight nonchalant shrug of her shoulders.

"Shut up, Sasha, you know you're pretty. But you better hurry up. They always do the Snowball first thing after the speeches."

"Do you think he'll pick me first?"

"Of course he'll pick you. The most popular boy always picks the most popular girl."

The tapping of high heels started up again; the girls were leaving.

The opening of the door brought the rhythmic beat of the hip-hop music back in, until it was quiet again.

"Oh no," Caroline said after a beat. "You're hiding from the Snowball dance, aren't you?"

The Snowball dance.

Also known as:

Ten Ways to Get a Girl to Hide in a Toilet Stall for Four Hours

1. Invent a party game where all the kids make a big circle around the kid whose party it is and have that kid choose his or her first partner from everyone who is standing there waiting to be picked. Or not. After they do that, everyone stands there and just watches them dance, until the DJ calls out, "Snowball," whereupon that couple breaks apart and each picks another person to dance with, and so on and so forth, until the last few kids are chosen because they are the only ones left.
2. Have a Bar or Bat Mitzvah party and hire a really loud, pushy DJ who will make sure all the kids who come have a great time by humiliating them and making them participate in said party game as described above.
3. Make sure there is one girl (in this case, Annie Diamond) who has a crush on the most popular boy in the grade (Matt Miller) whose Bar Mitzvah party it happens to be. Then have her standing in the aforementioned circle

knowing she will not only not be the first one picked but will mostly be the last.

Okay, that was only three, not ten. But still. Everything else was true. And everyone at school had been talking about it for weeks. The pressure had been building on both sides. Tensions were high.

"You think Matt's not going to pick you," Caroline said.

Annie nodded slowly.

"You think he's going to pick Sasha Binder."

Annie nodded again.

Matt had been in the pre-K program at the JCC. Annie went two days a week, and Matt went three, and the kids that went all five days kept getting them confused. It was understandable.

At four years old, Annie and Matt were almost exactly the same size. They both had short, curly, brown hair. They both wore red sneakers every day to school. It was most likely the red sneakers that was most confusing to the other four-year-olds. When Annie and Matt finally got to see each other at the Simchat Torah celebration, it was as if they were already friends. When the two moms also met and became best friends, it was inevitable. Annie and Matt fell in love with each other the way only five-, six-, and seven-year-olds can.

The problem was Annie never stopped.

"Oh, I'm *so* sorry. I wasn't even thinking." Caroline wrapped her arms around Annie.

They both sat down together, sharing the closed lid, their legs touching, their shoulders leaning against each other.

"I should have remembered," Caroline said.

"No." Annie shook her head. "I should have told you."

"Well, that's true. You should have told me. I'm your best friend."

The bathroom door opened again. The music swelled, heels clicked across the floor, no talking this time, the next stall over swung open, then shut, a lock slid into place, after a short while the toilet flushed, more footsteps, water running, a loud sigh, hand dryer blowing, music rushing in again, and then silence.

"Well, I'll wait here with you then," Caroline said.

"No, no," Annie said. She jumped up and unlocked the door. "You have to go out and see what's happening."

"But I don't like leaving you here."

"I'll be fine. Just let me know who he picks first, okay?"

Caroline nodded solemnly.

* * *

By the time Caroline returned to the bathroom stall, Annie had checked her Instagram no fewer than twelve times, closing it and opening it back up again, just to see if anyone from the party (no more than one hundred yards from where she was hiding) had posted any pictures of the Snowball dance. There were none.

"That's because they haven't done it yet," Caroline said, slipping back into the stall, this time locking the door herself.

"Why not?" Annie asked.

"I think there was something wrong with the DJ's microphone. They just got it working again and now Matt's dad is going to talk. Then I think Matt's grandfather is going to say something or do something. And then there's the dancing part, right?"

Annie sighed. "Right."

"You may be here for a while. Do you want me to bring you a plate?" Caroline asked. "I saw mini-hot dogs go by before."

"No, thanks. I don't feel like eating."

Just as Annie said that, the clarinet began the high-pitched starting notes of "Hava Nagila," the Hebrew song that means, "Come, let us rejoice and be happy."

"We're not really the party types anyway," Caroline said, sliding herself down next to Annie again.

"You don't *have* to have a party, you know?" Caroline said after a beat. "All you need to do is go up to the Torah and say a blessing. Everything else is optional."

"Really?"

"Really."

Annie would become a Bat Mitzvah next year, but she had already begun learning a lot about it. Oddly, it was only now, explaining these things to Caroline, who wasn't Jewish, that things started to make sense—like what it all actually meant. And suddenly the bathroom didn't feel as safe and comfortable as it had just a few minutes ago.

"It's the age you're supposed to act more grown up. Before,

everything you do is your parent's fault...well, responsibility, I mean."

Annie was starting to feel like *Alice in Wonderland*, when Alice took a bite of a cookie and began to grow and grow until her legs broke through the window of the tiny house.

"But after your Bar or Bat Mitzvah, it's on you. More or less."

"Like how?" Caroline asked.

"Well, like how you treat other people," Annie told Caroline—telling herself at the same time. "About how you are supposed to take care of the whole world really. Animals, the planet. It's not actually about what you do in front of everyone at the service, or how good you do or bad you mess up. It's what you do after that."

"So then I take it Snowball is not a requirement at a Bar Mitzvah?" Caroline joked.

But Annie still looked very serious.

"Oh, no," Caroline said. "I'm sorry. Too soon?"

"No." Annie broke into a smile. "Not soon enough. Let's get out of here."

✱ ✱ ✱

The hora was just winding down. From the looks of it, it had been a wild rumpus of rejoicing. Most of the men had their jackets off. Most of the boys were jacketless *and* tieless, and were swinging light sticks at each other like swords. The girls had taken off their dress shoes and were all wearing the little socks that had been passed around in a basket. Women's shawls and scarfs were hanging over the backs of chairs. And then the DJ announced it.

The Snowball dance.

The adults all took their seats, while a flurry of kids moved to the dance floor and formed a big circle of anticipation. No one looked particularly comfortable, least of all Matt, who stood in the center of everyone, picking at his nails. He looked nervous, the way he did at summer camp when they were ten and he had to take the deep-water test. Or the way he looked when they were in second grade together and he had to recite a poem by Shel Silverstein in front of the entire class. In other words, super cute. But not real happy.

"What do you want to do, Annie?" Caroline asked.

"I think I just want to watch." Annie sat down at a long table spread with chicken nuggets, M&Ms, discarded plastic garlands, and yes, mini-hot dogs.

Caroline sat down next to her. "Me too, then," she said.

Annie dipped a nugget into the honey mustard. "The party part's not bad either, you know," she said, then popped it into her mouth.

Caroline nodded and they both turned their chairs around for a better view of the dance floor.

"All righty then, young man. Who is going to be your first dance partner?"

Matt didn't move. He was looking around the circle. The DJ nudged him again, and Matt walked over to Sasha Binder. He kind of just stopped in front of where she was standing. The music began thumping, and that was that. Just like everyone expected.

Most popular boy. Most popular girl.

But what wasn't expected was that all Annie felt was huge relief. Snowball looked like the worst of gym class and musical chairs rolled into one.

Sure, it didn't feel good to see Matt and Sasha with their arms around each other taking tiny steps and swaying a tiny bit back and forth. Sasha took out her cell phone and snapped a selfie, but Matt was looking the other way. Then the DJ called out, "Snowball," and they broke apart.

It was really no big deal at all. Well, not as big a deal as Annie had worried it would be. Okay, it felt awful. But certainly not worth hiding in a bathroom stall at the Hyatt Regency in Stamford, Connecticut. Even if she really, really liked him. Which she did.

"C'mon." Annie stood up. She held out her hand to Caroline. "Let's dance."

* * *

"I'm really sorry," Matt said.

By ten thirty, parents were showing up to get their kids and head home. A few jackets were still on the floor, along with smushed remnants of cake, light sticks, a kippah or two, Hershey's Kisses wrappers, and quite a few abandoned white socks.

"For what?" Annie asked. Caroline had already been picked up.

Annie's mom had texted her that she would be a few minutes late. Most all the other kids were gone. Except, of course, for Matt.

His shirt had come undone, his tie was all crooked, and he had a smudge of what looked like chocolate frosting on his forehead, but he was still super cute. "For that stupid Snowball dance," Matt said.

"What do you mean?"

"You know we both hate that kind of thing. Remember second grade when I just had to recite that Shel Silverstein poem?"

"Remember when I totally flubbed up my book report in fourth grade?"

"Yeah, you totally started crying."

"Yeah, and so did you that time at summer camp. Deep water, remember?" Annie said. She flicked him on the forehead with her finger. That was their trademark.

He flicked her back. "Yeah, yeah, I remember," he said. Then he softened his voice and looked down at his feet. "I was looking for you, you know. But you weren't there."

"Where?" Annie asked.

"The Snowball dance."

"You were?"

"Yeah, I guess you were too smart to stand there like an idiot. Like me." Matt looked down at his shoes when he talked. "I think it's what I've always liked about you, Annie. You stand up for yourself. You don't do what everyone else is doing just because they are doing it."

Annie smiled. “Well, I don’t know about that,” she began.

“What do you mean?”

“It’s a long story.”

“I’ve got time.” Matt smiled back.

The Second Ever Bat Mitzvah of New York City

Barbara Bottner

Shy people should not be expected to go onstage and chant in Hebrew, while their every last muscle nervously vibrates for the entire world to see (or in my case, the Lower East Side). But this is my situation. I'm the first girl to be a Bat Mitzvah since Miss Judith Kaplan of the Upper West Side two years ago in 1922.

Judith, however, was *born* to this destiny. She's some kind of genius who learned to read English at age two and a half and began studying Hebrew at age three. She was a musical prodigy. At twelve, the little show-off read a passage from the weekly Torah portion in Hebrew *and* English from the printed Humash. Why did she have to go and do all of that? Obviously to put pressure on every other Jewish girl in this country!

Or because her father is a rabbi. As a rabbi's daughter, she probably *loves* learning about Judaism and being onstage to follow in his, Rabbi Mordecai's, footsteps.

"That little Kaplan girl is going places," said my mother when she read about her in the Jewish newspaper.

"Where's she going?" I asked. "Maybe she'll come downtown to join us in the Yiddish theater?"

"Don't be a smarty-pants, Hannah. Rich families don't like to see their daughters anywhere near the stage."

"Except at the bimah."

"The bimah is not exactly a stage. Anyway, her father broke with tradition. See, since ancient times, rabbinic Jews disapproved of theater for men and women alike. It was specifically considered immodest for women to perform for men."

"So you and the aunts break with tradition every night?" I asked, a little impressed.

We're in our family's Yiddish theater on Second Avenue, also known as the Jewish Rialto, which is where you can find me most of the time. After dinner I usually hang with my zeyde Zigmund, who's a sort of rabbi himself. Or rabbi type. We're sitting on the old couches we have here for actors to relax between scenes. My grandpa's carefully loading his pipe with tobacco, but his green eyes are glued onto me.

He says, "Shayna, you will sing, reflect, and interpret a passage. We'll all be listening. How you *feel* onstage has nothing to do with becoming a Bat Mitzvah. We'll be interested in what you *think*! You'll get so much out of it."

My name isn't Shayna, by the way, although everyone calls me that. Shayna means "beautiful." Nice, but my name is Hannah. Hannah means "grace." I'm neither beautiful nor graceful. I'm all ears and pimples and overbite; a typical almost-thirteen-year-old with uncontrollable hair that is unresponsive to creams or barrettes. But my family doesn't care how I look. They're dead set on parading me in front of the universe. *They're* all actresses, see? They *love* nothing more than being onstage. They crave the limelight.

Please, G-d, no.

G-d rarely listens to me. I know I have it all wrong; *I'm* supposed to listen to *G-d*. I listen, I do, especially first thing in the morning. Honestly, I don't think G-d is a morning Entity. Maybe He needs his coffee first, like my mom. In any case, I'm all ears, Dear Lord.

See, shyness is only one problem I have with going up to the bimah. I also worry if this Jewish G-d likes women at *all*; otherwise, we would have been all Bat Mitzvahed throughout the ages, right? My family is almost all female, except for my zeyde and my dad, Shlomo, who's rarely around. Neither one treats any of us like second-class citizens. But the Torah does. I'm semi-interested in the Torah, but as far as stories go, I prefer those I watch in the theater. For one thing, they have music. And dancing. And joy.

My zeyde is the one who's teaching me about Judaism. He usually smells of onions and chicken fat. I like his soulful eyes and his soft, rumbly voice. When it comes to the singing though, he can't carry a tune. Not even a little. He's tone deaf, yet *he's* teaching me the cantillation. Rabbis here on the Lower East Side are too busy with boys' Bar Mitzvahs to bother to help a girl out.

Unlike me, my grandfather is perfectly comfortable to be the most important person in the room, in *any* room. He's famous; he writes the plays my mom and her sisters perform. They also sing, dance, and choreograph. None of my aunts have children, so I'm the de facto daughter to them all. My dad has a shop in the garment center. He makes our costumes. And he prays a lot, like all the men we know.

I think G-d skipped over me in the talent department. Yet, as I've explained, He made me a wise guy. I mean wise *girl*. Isn't it strange there's a word for great men, *mensch*, but none for great women? That's what I mean about G-d! And yet, I have to sing *His* praises. Why is that? Isn't He the Most Powerful Force in the Universe? What does He care what *I*, a skinny almost-thirteen-year-old, think of *Him*? If he were a person like my next-door neighbor Moshe, I wouldn't want to have to go around saying, "Moshe, you're the Lord Almighty, King of the Universe." How creepy would that be?

This is why I wish I could worship a goddess. I see my aunts and mother as goddesses, goddesses of the Yiddish Theater. Their photos are in the newspapers all the time. But we can't have any images of G-d. There's so much I don't understand.

Fact: no matter what my zeyde says, *not* wanting to recite my haftarah is *all* I can think about.

That is, when I *can* think.

Together, my mom and her sisters own this building. Our theater seats about a hundred people. We all live above it in a bunch of different apartments. I do my homework backstage because I have a job. Jobs. I'm the assistant costumer, assistant hairdresser, and assistant stage manager. In other words, I barely find time to sit down. I work with the prop person (my aunt Adele), locate everyone's outfits, and drag them into their dressing rooms. Some are so heavy I fall over just trying to get them where they belong. I'm the seamstress too; I take these musty dresses in with pins if they are too large and let them out if they're too small. Mostly, they're too small because Jews love to eat and Ratner's deli is close by on Delancey Street. Most nights, we go there after our show because we're all zinging with energy. We're lucky that it stays open until 2:00 a.m. Lots of the theater people are there too, ordering chopped chicken liver or boiled cabbage soup and freshly baked rye bread and downing barrels of pickles—the pickles are free.

Theater people love free food because they're never paid enough in wages, so they're generally hungry.

This is who I've seen at Ratner's: Molly Picon in her stage makeup, Paul Muni trying to toast with a raspy voice. I've given Joseph Buloff extra coleslaw and hailed a cab for Bina Abramowitz. Celia Adler asked me to please bring her mustard, and Mina Bern was in the ladies' room at the same time as I was.

These famous actors pinch my cheeks and talk about me in

Yiddish, thinking I don't understand a word, but I know tons: schlemiel (a bungler), chochem (a wise man), klutz (an awkward person), chutzpah (brazen), kvetch (complain), mensch (a real good guy), schmooze (talk or gossip), schmatta (a dress), tuchus (your bum), schnorrer (a freeloader), farbrecher (crook), meshuga (crazy). Yiddish is the most colorful language ever. I love that there are hundreds of ways to call someone a jerk. I know them all.

Don't get me started.

"Schmaltz [chicken fat] brings everyone together!" Tonight, my favorite aunt, Adele, toasts everyone with root beer. She's dark-haired, with eyes that infect you with exuberance. She's gorgeous and sings really well. My mother, Rose, the oldest, is the director. Her four sisters—Pearl, Natalie, Minnie, and Adele—all dance and sing and act.

So naturally, I love the Yiddish theater. It makes life so intense. It's the best way to learn about our people escaping from Europe, fleeing oppression. *And* our customs and even love lives. We Jews have a great sense of humor and irony. And powerful spirits. This I learned from plays, not the Torah. I don't think there are any jokes in the Torah, but there are plenty in the theater.

My dreaded Bat Mitzvah, which is dead serious, is two months away.

Everyone knows my mother is a big feminist but not a big Jew, so I was shocked when she decided *I* was to be a Bat Mitzvah. "We have a theater run by women. We built this from nothing. You know more than most girls how smart and powerful females are. Being called to the bimah is a great honor. You'll make us so proud. Time to step up."

"Aren't you proud of me already? Is this conditional love, Mom?"

"*Stop* being a smarty-pants, Hannah!"

"Here's my problem. G-d is male. He never answers my prayers."

"G-d has no gender, Hannah. Or I should say He has dual gender. We say 'He' but it's shorthand. G-d is as female as He/She is male. Having a Bat Mitzvah will educate you to halakhah. So you can teach others."

"Halakhah?"

"Jewish law. Did you know in the Ketubah, the marriage ceremony, it says the wife is obliged to teach the husband the Torah?"

"Did you teach Dad?"

"I keep meaning to, honey, but I've been too busy. With *you*! But you see what G-d entrusted women to do? That is a huge endorsement for us."

"Okay. But, Ma, I want to stay backstage and help put the show on."

"I know, honey. And you do a great job. We depend on you."

Fact: I sing, but being shy, I sing to myself, often in the closet or walking down Houston Street when I go to pick up bialys for everyone. I love being around my family. They're playful and silly and love to laugh. They do this thing called improvisation, which means they invent stories and characters right in the moment.

Fact: I wish one of these talented performers could present my haftarah. They're all hams. Which is good because according to my mother, Jews in this new country need to laugh. "We lived in shtetls. We came from the villages with one dress, one jacket, and one pair of shoes. We had to leave behind our parents and grandparents, brothers and sisters, knowing they might not survive the pogroms. Thank G-d we're storytellers." She looks at me. "Your haftarah is a story too! You should be so happy to stay in the family business. Telling your story means it will survive. That's how we know what happened in ancient times."

"*You* didn't have to get a Bat Mitzvah and learn to read Hebrew!"

"Would you rather do it in Yiddish?" She pokes me in the stomach.

"Ouch! *No!* Every time I try to speak Yiddish, I get a sore throat."

She shakes her head and hands me a needle and thread and nods toward a hem that's ripped. "You'll do fine. Just gargle and blow your nose first."

The deal I made with my mother is this: I'd help her with the costumes and the grunt work backstage as long as she'd promise *never* to push me out on the stage. So I dutifully dump the ashtrays filled with butts and tissues with makeup on them; I change the light bulbs around the mirrors. I keep the place clean. I do my part.

Anyway, she promised.

And re-promised.

And re-re-promised.

But thanks to Miss Judith Kaplan, now I have to renegotiate all over again. This makes me want to take the trolley uptown and drag Judith downtown. Fair is fair.

My zeyde says that the Bat Mitzvah ceremony will be a marker of Jewish Adulthood for me. He says this as if I should be thrilled.

"But you always say I'm immature. So why *rush* things?"

He sighs. "I remember when you didn't want to learn to brush your teeth. I also remember when you didn't want to go to kindergarten. When you refused to cross the street for the first time. Take a trolley. Now, you do all those things. You'll do this too."

"But I didn't have to do those things in *front of an audience*! People waiting for me to mess up. Honestly, could you brush your teeth if a hundred people were watching?"

"First the uppers, then the lowers."

"Very funny."

"Then rinse."

I smell the sweet, pungent tobacco smoke rising off his pipe. He's not allowed to smoke in the kitchen. He knows it but he does anyway. He's the big macher of the family. The big deal.

"Shayna, the children of Israel had to wander around the wilderness for forty years, a journey which should have taken them weeks. But they'd been slaves for four hundred years. They needed to grow *out* of their slave consciousness in order to have the maturity to create an ethical society. At times there was no food or water. They lost confidence in their leader. They yearned to go back to Egypt, where they had the security of knowing what came next. Before they were ready to fulfill their dreams, they needed to face themselves and grow up as a people. *That's* what this ritual is about.

Growing up. Being scared but overcoming."

"In four hundred years I'd get mature too!"

"You get a month, honey."

He opens the book, but I'm distracted. I hear the piano coming from the stage. It's Aunt Adele imitating Eddie Cantor singing "If You Knew Susie." I start to hum under my breath." 'If you knew Susie, like I knew Susie, oh, oh, oh what a gal…'"

"Do you want to sing 'If You Knew Susie' instead of your Torah portion and haftarah, Hannah?" He starts singing too. Like I said, he's got a tin ear.

"*Stop*, Grandpa!"

"You have a sweet soprano voice, Shayna. Let's use it for your haftarah. You should read the Book of Judges for background."

He hands me the book and I read:

"Sisera, a general, led King Jabin's Canaanite army against Israel. Deborah, a priestess, declared that King Jabin must be defeated; his troops must be delivered to Israel. She predicted that Sisera would fall 'by the hand of a woman.' Jael is a woman warrior. When exhausted, Sisera sleeps in Jael's tent, thinking Jael's an ally, and she betrays him; she takes a pin to his head and hammers it in."

Talk about drama.

"Wow! Jael was fearless!"

"That's why it's a good section for you to read. You're also fearless."

"Uh, Deborah led an entire army. I can't even go onstage."

"You think it was easy? That Deborah woke up one morning, got her tea, and thought, *Hmm, nice spring morning! A fine day to go to war?*"

"Depends on the tea, I guess."

Well, that was the day my zeyde convinced me my haftarah was worth learning, if I could get over hating the idea of being onstage. Which I did, in an unexpected way.

One Sunday afternoon we were about to debut a new show. Before I began to study with Grandpa, I had run lines with my aunts. The dress rehearsal went really well. But my mother was suddenly running around howling like a madwoman. "Adele has a fever! She *has* to stay in bed. I need a singing prostitute for the second act!" Her eyes landed on my face.

"Why are you looking at me, Ma? I'm your daughter. A very serious Jewish scholar, certainly *not* a singing prostitute. Not a prostitute at all, which I'm sure you know."

"Honey, for just one night, couldn't you be a singing prostitute? The costume is adorable!"

"I think that's child endangerment, Ma."

"Stop being a wiseass. *Please?*"

"You want *me* to go onstage? In a prostitute's costume? *And* sing?"

"You won't be *you*, honey. You'll be a character."

She handed me the outfit. It was my color. It fit perfectly. My aunt Pearl appeared out of nowhere and started dabbing on makeup. "Shayna, you look so grown up. And gorgeous."

"Can you cover my pimples at least?"

"My pleasure. And I'm going to give you rouge and lipstick. And blue eyeshadow. Take a look at your future, doll." She held up a mirror.

"I'm not planning a career in prostitution, Aunt Pearl."

Here's the big surprise. I looked gorgeous. Who knew? I'd never worn makeup in my life.

My aunt Minnie looked me over and said: "You're the spitting image of your aunt Adele at your age."

My mother gave me the script. "Memorize these lines." She dragged me into one of the stuffed chairs. I rehearsed every word. The next thing I knew, we had intermission and it was time for the second act. Someone dragged me to stage right and pushed me out there. The floodlights hit my eyes and for a minute I could barely see. Then I heard my mother hiss: *"Line!"*

I said it. And I continued to the next line. Then I was dancing with the other prostitutes. I knew the choreography. The song had a chorus, and I belted out the words. I have a pretty strong soprano and my voice sailed over the audience. I mean, I *nailed* that song.

Then I heard laughter. I didn't understand. It wasn't a funny song.

Oh! I realized I was onstage *alone. All* alone! The scene had ended, and the violin had played a few more notes. Everyone else had left for the wings—everyone but me. What was I supposed to do now? Run? There was incredible applause though. I mean tumultuous. What to do? I bowed. And then I bowed again. I was out there, so why not? I blew kisses to the audience. They loved it.

Then I heard my mother whisper: "*Leave*, stage right. *Exit!*"

I did. But all I could think was, *I want to go back out there!*

"See, she's *not* adopted," said my aunt Pearl backstage. "She's one of us after all."

My zeyde spun me around. "See how G-d loves you? He gave your aunt Adele a tiny little cold so you could have the opportunity to overcome your fears. Now you've crossed the desert and you can build yourself a new country. The country of Deborah. And Jael. The country of Hannah. The country of courage."

So you can see why I studied with my zeyde.

In the end, when I stood on the bimah, I had so much to say about my haftarah: how you can be a warrior even if you don't have an army behind you; how you have to face enemies *inside* of you like doubt and avoidance and fear. We can't all be Judith Kaplans, but we all have strength and insight. And talent too. Sometimes it takes a while to find it, although we should probably not let it go unnoticed for forty years.

The absolute truth is my Bat Mitzvah was the talk of the Lower East Side. My zeyde asked me if I thought it would make a good play.

I said, "Maybe. If you could cast an up-and-coming star of the Yiddish Theater."

He knew exactly what I meant.

Helping Noah: A Torah Travel Adventure

Stacia Deutsch

"Want to skateboard to temple today, Simon?" my sister Jody asked. We both knew that was a joke. Our moms had gotten me a fancy penny board for my birthday in the hope I'd want to try it. They even gave me a helmet and kneepads, but people get hurt on skateboards. The board, in its original box, lay under my bed.

At my stare, she moaned, "Fine. I'll drive you."

This conversation was predictable.

Once we were on the way, I grasped my Hebrew notebook tightly in two fists and, just like I had every Wednesday for the last six months, asked, "Can you drive more carefully?"

Just like every other time, she playfully revved the engine to irritate me, then careened into the temple parking lot, jolting to a stop.

"Thanks for the ride," I said sarcastically. I sighed, relieved that this was my very last tutoring appointment with the rabbi. My Bar Mitzvah was Saturday. Four more days, then I'd be free.

I opened the door of her junkie death mobile.

"You'll need your backpack today," Jody said, swinging it out the window. I was pretty sure I'd left the pack in the house, so I didn't understand why she had it.

"I have everything I need right here," I told her, waving my Hebrew folder.

"Take it." Jody tossed the backpack on the temple lawn and began to peel away but then reversed to me. "Tell Elizabeth I said good luck today. We're all counting on you both."

My sister had said a lot of strange things in the thirteen years I'd known her, but this was top of the list. There was a lot to decipher. Elizabeth Stone lived next door to us. We weren't friends. To me, she always seemed confident and brave. She raised her hand a lot in class. Basically, that meant the only thing we had in common was that her Bat Mitzvah was last week and my Bar Mitzvah was this Saturday. Elizabeth had invited me to her party, but I don't like parties, so I didn't go.

Now Jody wanted me to tell our overachieving neighbor good luck. For what?

Then there was the added, "We're counting on you both." What on earth was that?

I'd have asked my questions, but Jody's car spun out of the parking lot before I could say anything. I stood there for a moment listening to the engine rattle fade when a piercing bark nabbed my attention. A small black dog pulled its owner around the corner. It might have been a poodle or possibly a shrunken pit bull. To me, all dogs looked the same, semi-evolved wolf descendants, and even though this one was on a leash, it still had teeth. I grabbed my backpack and, clutching my Hebrew folder, ran as fast as my legs could carry me into the building.

"The rabbi isn't here today." A stranger was in the rabbi's office, sitting at her desk.

I glanced back at the door. "Should I call my sister?" I never took my phone to temple, so I'd need permission to call from the office. "She's my ride." Jody'd be back in half an hour, but I didn't want to wait around if tutoring was canceled.

"You can't leave," the stranger said. "You have work to do."

"I'm ready," I replied. "I know my Torah reading. I have the prayers memorized. Speech is solid. I've even finished my mitzvah project." At first, it might seem unlike me to have done a fundraiser for the local animal shelter, but keeping stray dogs off the street was a personal mission, if not a slight obsession. A win-win.

Without a word, the stranger pointed at the empty chair across from the rabbi's desk. I tightened my grip around my Hebrew folder, which contained copies of the prayers plus my speech, and sat. In the silence, I studied the stranger's reflection in a window.

Short hair. Thick glasses. Dark eyes. And when the stranger smiled, there was something in that grin that made me shiver.

"There's the matter of the flood," the stranger said, then paused, as if waiting for me to reply.

"What flood?" I asked. The weather was forecast to be perfectly clear the day of my service. "It'll be sixty-three degrees. And sunny."

The stranger didn't blink. "You need to go now, Simon." Adding, "No matter what happens, do not get on the boat."

This was too weird. I felt uncomfortable, so I said, "Sure. No boat. Okay. Bye." I was happy to be getting out of there even if it meant waiting for Jody in the parking lot.

I walked through the rabbi's office door, and that's when everything turned upside down.

One minute, I was leaving my rabbi's office…the next, I was standing in the rain.

✡ ✡ ✡

I was inside my Torah portion.

How did I know?

Well, since I'd read the text in Hebrew and English about a thousand times, I knew Noah's story really well. The clues were there: first, the torrential downpour. My freshly cut Bar Mitzvah hair was drooping into my eyes. I was sure I looked like a wet, fuzzy, brown puppy. And all things puppy are bad.

If that wasn't convincing enough, I'd say the enormous ark in front of me was a sure sign.

Apparently, this was what the Biblical reference to building the ark from "gopher wood" meant. It looked like normal wood to me. I'd also wondered about the measurement called "cubits," and now I was definitely looking at about three hundred of them lengthwise, fifty wide, and thirty high. All those cubits together made a darned big boat. The entrance was on the side. There was a ramp to get in. All details from the Torah.

I pinched myself to see if I was dreaming. Or nightmare-ing.

A voice said, "I've been waiting for you."

I turned. "Elizabeth?" My next-door neighbor stood beside me. Her blond hair was drenched. She wore waders and tall boots. *Someone* was prepared for rain.

"Do you have your gear?" she asked, as if I should have known to pack supplies. She pointed at my backpack.

"Uh..." I checked my bag. The answer to that was, oddly, "Yes." Turned out that Jody had stuffed my backpack for just this occasion, leaving me to wonder how she knew I'd need flood supplies.

I put away my Hebrew notebook and grabbed my raincoat. I switched out my tennis shoes for my boots, still stunned that *this* is where I was and unclear about what I was doing here.

We moved to a wooded spot where the branches were thick enough to slow the rainfall. I asked Elizabeth, "What's going on?"

She gave me a confident look. "We have to help Noah." At my confused stare, she asked, "You didn't think he could do it alone, did you?"

How was I supposed to answer that? Pretending for the moment that the story in the Torah was real, I said, "Noah has sons, sons' wives, and a wife of his own." I added, "First mentioned in Genesis 6, verse 18," just because I knew.

"Does it say anywhere in the text that they actually help him?" Elizabeth asked, which was a good point. "As far as I can tell, from my own quick Bible review, the guy has a ton of work and lives in a world full of rotten people who won't lend a hand." Even with the rain gear and the tree cover, we were getting super wet. Rain dripped off Elizabeth's chin as she said, "Noah needs us."

"Impossible," I told her. Followed by, "This is definitely a nightmare." I'll admit the cold felt cold and rain felt wet, so I said, "If there's carpentry left to be done, count me out. It's not in my skill set."

"Oh, the ark looks done to me," Elizabeth said boldly. "I'm pretty sure we're in stage two now." She grinned. "Or as you might say, Genesis 6, verse 19."

I didn't have to think about it. "That would be the line about gathering the ani—" Just then, the ground shook. The trees above us quivered, dropping sheets of rain off their broad, thick leaves. A trumpet rattled my bones. I recognized the animal's call from a nature show on TV.

"Get moving, you big lump of useless clay!" a bearded man shouted from the ark. His voice was muffled by the rain but still clear enough for us to hear. The guy stood on the third deck, leaning on the railing. Even from where we stood, which was pretty far off seeing as the boat was so big, I could tell his tattered robe was drenched.

"I hope you don't think I am going to save your sorry gray butt! Go find your lady elephant and come back when you have her! No one boards till everyone has their partner." His voice echoed as it carried on the wind. "If I see you by yourself one more time, I'm letting you drown!" He turned from the elephant and stomped off the deck.

"Wow! That speech wasn't in the Torah," I said, surprised not only that Noah was speaking English, but also that he was such a grumpy old man.

Elizabeth explained that while we were here, language was universal. She said that whatever we needed to communicate would come easily. That was helpful but didn't explain Noah's crummy attitude.

"The text says Noah was righteous," I said, wiping water from my eyes and staring at the ark. I suddenly realized what the Torah text meant. In writing my Bar Mitzvah speech, I'd mistakenly thought that "righteous" meant he was a good man. I'd written all about how we should aspire to be "righteous" like Noah. Big mistake.

From where I stood, it was clear that the word "righteous" in the Torah simply meant that Noah was the least bad dude in a world full of people who were really, really awful. The bar for being good enough to survive the flood was super low.

A foul smell reminded me that the elephant was still nearby. If a barking dog made me want to run, a trumpeting elephant was a zillion times worse. I almost would have preferred facing cranky Noah than an elephant. *Almost.*

"Why's the big gray guy still here?" I whispered to Elizabeth. I stood frozen, not daring to move.

The elephant trumpeted. Elizabeth trumpeted back. The elephant trumpeted again. "Our ability to process language doesn't just apply to people. Once you get used to it, you'll be able to understand the animals too. This elephant is telling us that his female friend is being stubborn. So I told him that we're going to help him bring her along. He said he'd give us a ride…" She moved closer to the elephant, who lowered his trunk toward her. Elizabeth swung casually onto the trunk, and he settled her down onto his back. "Come on, Simon."

"No. Negative. Nope. No way. Nada. Nil." There wasn't a chance I was getting on the back of that elephant. "Nyet," I added in Russian, just to make it crystal clear.

From high on the elephant's back, Elizabeth pointed toward the woods behind me. "Other animals surround us, all waiting to board the ark." It was then that I noticed movement in the trees and saw two giraffes. Two bears. A pair of turtles. Foxes. Eagles. Moose. Moose-es? Meese?

"There are two tigers behind that thorny bush if you'd like to stay here," Elizabeth told me. "I'm like eighty percent certain they aren't hungry." I swear a tiger growled just then.

"I'd prefer you tell me how to get home," I said, raising my hands in a karate stance, as if that might scare a tiger off.

"Simon," Elizabeth said, "have you noticed it's already raining?"

I didn't even bother to answer. It was an absurd question. Water dripped into my ears. She went on, "This is your Torah portion, so tell me, what happens when the rain starts to fall?"

Again, didn't have to think about it. The answer rolled off my tongue. "The ark is loaded, door closed, and it floats safely away, of course."

She pointed over at the ark. "This is the flood, Simon, and no animals are on that ark." She added, "Yet."

Water pooled around my ankles. Elizabeth was right. It wouldn't be long before the water reached my knees.

I squinted at the ark. It should have been bustling with activity, ready to float off toward the horizon. But instead there was Noah, all alone, lying in a hammock on deck two, under a little water-resistant gazebo made of leaves and wood. It looked like he was napping. Disappointment coursed through me. Noah was not righteous at all. I was going to have to revise my Bar Mitzvah speech. If I ever got to give it.

"What if we don't help him?" I asked Elizabeth. That elephant lowered its trunk for me to climb aboard. With a shivering breath, I moved away.

"The flood ends the world," Elizabeth said simply.

"Are you kidding?!" I asked, though she didn't seem like the type to joke around about stuff like that.

"I've drawn this conclusion," she said, "based on what Eitan told me last week when we helped create the world. He said if we didn't set things right, the world wouldn't exist anymore. I figure the same rules apply here."

Eitan Goldstone was my best friend. He hadn't mentioned traveling into Elizabeth's Torah portion with her. Or into his own last month, either. Eitan liked making up stories about things, and while I often forgot them the second he was finished, I'd have remembered these.

The message in Elizabeth's stare was clear. If I didn't get on the elephant and help gather animals for the ark, the end of the world would be my fault.

Elephant…Global Devastation…Elephant…TOTAL WORLD DESTRUCTION.

"Oh fine. Elephant," I sputtered, noting that I wasn't happy to be going along.

An elephant's trunk isn't like a broad platform; it's more like a thick tightrope. I decided standing up was for someone with more guts than I had, so I sat down, allowing Jumbo to wrap his trunk around me like a seat belt. I held on to the wrinkled, rough skin, praying my hands wouldn't slip in the rain as he lifted me off the ground.

The lift wasn't smooth. It was jarring and bumpy, and I was so scared that I had my eyes closed the whole time. And yet, when I settled behind Elizabeth on the high back of that elephant, I felt pretty proud that I'd gotten there.

My pride disappeared entirely when we began to move.

"AUGHHHH!" I screamed with every fiber of my soul as he hurried off in a stomping, lumbered gallop that threatened to throw me to my death with every step.

When Jumbo finally stopped, I could not get off fast enough, and as my feet hit the muddy ground, I wondered if there was another way back to the ark. Flood water was now lapping the middle of my shins and my fear was an eleven on a scale of one to ten.

"Remind me what we have to do?" I asked Elizabeth, since all memory had been jostled out of my brain. "And more important, once we do it—can we go home?"

"Save the world and yes," she said. Her confidence gave me confidence.

"Okay," I said with a huge breath. "Let's get Jumbo a friend."

"Jumbo?" Elizabeth asked.

"Do you have a better name?" I chuckled. The area where we stood was turning into a shallow lake. At first, I didn't see another elephant, but when I turned completely around, I found Jumbo reaching his long trunk out toward what appeared to be a muddy lump. The lump moved.

"Simon!" Elizabeth called to me. "The cow"—I knew that was the term for a female elephant—"is stuck."

"Of course she is," I moaned. I decided to look in my backpack just in case Jody had thought to give me a few more supplies, like rope or a forklift. Nothing but my Hebrew notebook, and that wasn't going to help us here.

"What do we do?" I asked Elizabeth, who I now noticed stood a good, safe distance away.

"My job is to figure out the problem. Since it's your Torah portion, you get to solve it," she said. "So what do *you* think, Simon?"

"Frankly, I thought you were leading this entire mission," I told her.

"Nope," she said, pointing toward Jumbo and his friend. "Your Bar Mitzvah. Your elephant."

"Is that what Eitan said to you last week?" I challenged.

"Yes," she replied. "Eitan said Jasmine said that Michael told her 'a madrich, your guide, arrives in the story early to help figure out the problem, then disappears at the hardest part of solving it.' That way, the Bar or Bat Mitzvah kid has to prove themselves alone." She explained, "When Jasmine vanished, Eitan nearly failed." She shook her head. "But in the end, he saved the world by himself."

So this was how it worked. Each Bar or Bat Mitzvah student helped the one after to navigate their Torah portion. I thought about which Torah portion came next and who had their Shabbat service the following weekend, when I noticed Elizabeth biting her lips. She muttered, "I wonder why I'm still here."

"Maybe someone out there knows that I'd mess up by myself," I said, totally serious. There was no way I could get two elephants on the ark alone. If I didn't think I'd sound pathetic, I'd have begged Elizabeth to never leave.

"I guess I'm still on guide duty. We're going to have to lift the elephant up and help her stand," Elizabeth said with the same conviction she always showed in class.

Water reached my knees and mud stained my pants. My heart thumped so hard, I thought I might faint when I followed Elizabeth behind the cow.

"Just be a good elephant. Please, don't sit on me, fall on me, or poop on me." I put my hands on the cow's butt and pushed. She didn't move. I scooted to the side and shoved at her with all my might while Elizabeth tugged her tusks.

I had to stay focused, or I'd have run away screaming. The elephant was massive, and I'd never get used to the smell. I wanted a hot shower, warm clothes, and to never leave home again.

"On the count of three," Elizabeth told me. "We're going to shove with everything we've got." She counted. "One, two…" And then, just like we weren't even there at all, the elephant yawned, stretched, and stood up. Elizabeth and I fell backward into the mud and muck.

"Did it work? Did we set the world straight?" I asked as the cow joined Jumbo in a less muddy part of the field.

"Uh, we're both still here," Elizabeth noted.

"Hmm." I took her hand and together we managed to drag ourselves up onto a rock. Jumbo and Mrs. Jumbo trumpeted joyfully.

"That was hard," I said, "but honestly, I am not sure we did anything. She seemed to just get up when she was ready."

"I think she was being stub—" Elizabeth began when suddenly she began to fade. When I say "fade," I mean she became kind of cloudlike, and then inch-by-inch, pieces of her began to disappear.

"Wait! Elizabeth!" I shouted when she was just a head, neck, and shoulders. "What's going on?"

"I was wrong, Simon," she said, her voice was a ghostly whisper in the windy rain. "It doesn't look like saving the elephant was what you had to do here today." She seemed incredibly sad. And maybe a little nervous to be leaving me.

"What am I supposed to do?" I could barely hear her.

Elizabeth's fading shoulders shrugged at me and then she entirely vanished.

It was exactly like she'd said earlier, "The madrich disappears at the hardest part."

Lightning flashed, and with it, I had a blinding flash of clarity.

Saving the world, and doing it alone, was not something I could do. It wasn't the noble choice, but I had to quit. With a resigned groan, I flopped onto the ground and let the water reach my chest. I stared into space, looking for a sign that this was a dream and I'd wake up. Or that a rescue was on the way…certainly the stranger in the rabbi's office knew I'd failed…

At the end of my Torah portion, Noah sees a rainbow, which meant everything would be okay. It wasn't like I saw a big arching rainbow like that, but a little ray of sunlight refracted through a tiny drop of rain on the tip of my nose and colors appeared.

Red. Orange. Yellow. I thought about my family, my friends, and honestly, it was like my whole life flashed before my eyes. I forced myself to stand up.

Green. Blue. I thought about Noah's ark and how the rainbow was a covenant, a promise. Total world destruction would never happen like this again. This was a one-time-only flood apocalypse. I straightened my spine and gathered courage that I'd never had before. I had to get back to the ark.

Indigo. Violet. Being righteous didn't mean you had to be a perfect person. It meant doing the right thing when the odds were not in your favor. It meant trying your best. It meant not giving up. I was going to save the world.

At least, I'd try really hard.

I trumpeted to Mrs. Jumbo and she agreed to carry me back to Noah's Ark. Now that the elephant had a mate, all species were present and accounted for. The animals lined up, two by two, ready to float safely away. Only, the door was closed and Noah, cruise director and captain, was nowhere to be found.

The ark began to sway as the flood lifted it off the ground. If the animals didn't board soon, they'd all… Nope! Nyet! Not if I could help!

Think, Simon, think. The story goes that Noah, his kids and their wives, and Noah's wife went into the ark. That was Genesis 7, verse 1. Then in verses 2 and 3 the birds and beasts boarded. Verse 4 was the flood. The same story repeats in verse 7, with animals in 8 and 9, and the flood in 10. And then repeated one more time, with Noah and his family getting on in verse 13, animals after, and the inevitable flood in 17.

The order must have been important, seeing as the whole thing was repeated over and over. I knew what I needed to do.

* * *

"Get on the boat," I told Noah when I found him in his village hut. He was fixing himself a pomegranate and olive sandwich while his bed and couch floated back and forth with the tide.

"Go away," he snarled at me. "I'd rather face the flood than be cooped up with a maddening zoo for forty days and forty nights."

I recognized what Noah was feeling 100 percent. I never wanted to do anything that involved risk or any sort of danger, and let's not forget I was the one who did a selfish charity project to get stray dogs off the street so that they couldn't bite *me*! I was also the one who, if Elizabeth hadn't been there, never would have tried to shove an elephant, never mind ride one.

"You're scared," I told him.

"Am not," Noah said, just as I would have.

"Are too," I said. "You taunted the elephants, but the truth is you don't want them to get on the ark, because if they do, you have to go too."

"What difference does it make?" Noah asked. "No matter what, everyone I know will be gone by morning." That was depressing, but if Noah didn't get on the ark, everyone I knew would be gone by morning too.

"This is the one and only Earth-cleansing flood," I assured him. And for the first time, he seemed to notice that I was a stranger.

"Who are you?" he asked, squinting at me.

"Someone who is grateful you survive," I told him. Just then, Noah's wife, three sons, and their wives entered the hut.

Noah's wife looked at me and echoed, "Who are you?"

I didn't answer. "I need you all to get on the ark." I added, "Now."

His family seemed ready, but Noah said, "I'm not going."

I remembered that Noah was the least bad person in his generation, which meant he was still pretty darned bad. So I said, "I'll make you a deal. Get on the boat, and when the flood is over, you can have a big party." That was pretty much what happened anyway. After the flood, Noah drank too much wine and fell asleep naked on a beach.

"I'll go if you go," Noah told me. "That's *my* deal."

I had been told not to get on the ark, but now I had no choice. Ignoring the warning quiver in my belly, I said, "Deal."

Noah led the way. I forced myself to stay right behind him, so every time he looked over his shoulder, I was right there.

We entered the ark, which, I'll admit, was pretty nice inside. Noah had done a good job with the construction, a big accomplishment since there were so few guidelines other than the wood and the cubits.

"This is cool," I complimented. Noah rolled his eyes.

Once he was on board with his family, the animals cheerfully bounded up the gangplank.

I worried they'd eat each other. Or they'd eat Noah and his family.

Or they'd eat me. They didn't. Oddly, they didn't seem to need to eat. Or poop. They were still smelly, but as far as animals on a floating zoo goes, it could have been worse.

Once the ark was loaded, I breathed a huge sigh of relief and said, "See ya." I headed for the exit. Now, I'd finished everything required for my Bar Mitzvah, including saving the world, so I assumed I'd be sucked up into space rather quickly, just like Elizabeth. I just had to get off the boat.

"You got me into this," Noah declared. "You're seeing it through to the end." He shut and sealed the main door. "If anything goes wrong, I blame you."

Did I mention that Noah was the *most righteous guy* in his entire generation?

The boat drifted, and I began to panic. This was bad. Really bad. I was *on* the ark!

I took several deep breaths and analyzed my situation:

Noah was complaining about everything he could complain about.

His kids—not righteous either—were poking the bears with sticks.

The wives—also not righteous—were telling nasty stories that I'd never repeat.

All I knew was that I had to get off the ark. So I snuck past them to go to the third deck and out into the pouring rain. The place where Elizabeth and I had stood was completely under the ocean.

Horror surged through me as I watched the last speck of dry land get farther and farther away.

I heard Jumbo trumpet from the deck below. Followed by a second trumpet, a roar, and a growl. I didn't need a translation to know that the animals were encouraging me to abandon ship. I bravely climbed onto the ark's railing.

Noah appeared. "Where are you going?" He lunged to grab my raincoat.

"The madrich disappears at the hardest part," I said calmly, and then I dove off the deck into the swirling water.

* * *

I was outside the temple. My clothes were dry. My boots and raincoat were inside my backpack. There was a honk as my sister's car sped into the lot and skidded to a stop.

"How was tutoring?" she asked when I opened the door.

"How fast can you drive?" I answered.

Jody tossed back her head and laughed. I didn't nag at her or complain about her driving the whole way home. Before she even parked in the driveway, I jumped out of the car and ran next door. Elizabeth opened the door before I rang the bell.

"Hi," Elizabeth said. She seemed relieved, and happy, to find me there. She started, "I'm sorry, Simon. I'm not used to messing up—"

"Uh." I glanced around as if someone might be listening. "Are we supposed to talk about this…after?"

"I guess not," Elizabeth said. "Though I'd really like to process—"

"Can't." I shook my head. Generations of kids, maybe even before the invention of the Bar and Bat Mitzvah, had done what I did. My moms, their parents, back and back and back—who knew how far it went? We all had a role to play in keeping the past safe and protecting the future. And we had to keep the secret.

I told Elizabeth, "I'm changing my entire speech. Noah might have been the most righteous in his generation, but I think we can do better in ours." Then, I switched the subject. "Do you like skateboarding?"

"I don't know," she said, revealing an uncertainty I'd never heard before. And a tinge of curiosity.

"I have a penny board. Maybe we can try it together?" I asked.

"I'm up to the *tusk*. Are you?" Elizabeth winked.

✱ ✱ ✱

That night, I pulled out my family's tattered old Bible. Lech L'cha was the story that came after Noah's Ark. It was about Abraham and Sarah and their journey. I glanced over at my rain boots stashed in the corner of my room and thought, *I'll need hiking boots.*

This Is What I'll Tell You

Debbie Reed Fischer

September 1, 1980

Dear Diary,

How am I supposed to sleep tonight? I can't stop thinking about tomorrow. Even though I've been "that new kid" before (five times, to be exact), this time it's *way* different. It's seventh grade, as in JUNIOR HIGH, with tons of classrooms and hallways to learn. I'm definitely, positively, absolutely going to get lost. On top of that, it's not like a school in the States, where I'd know what to wear. How do people dress in Greece? I mean, I know there's going to be some American kids, but what if I can't find them?

Worst of all, what if everyone finds out I'm Jewish?

I can't let that happen.

I need a plan. Dad always says Proper Preparation Prevents Poor Performance. He calls it the Five P's.

Prep List for First Day at American International School of Athens

Jeans: Nothing show-offy. I'll go with the Levi's Mom bought at the BX on base. Other Air Force brats will be wearing the same pair, so it will signal I'm one of them, not a civilian or State Department kid. Maybe they'll see my jeans and invite me to eat lunch with them.

Actually, I won't wait for them to invite me. I've got to be BRAVE. Introduce myself. Make a friend on day one. Be seen and heard and let people get to know me. I *have* to make this different from last year.

Hide my Star of David necklace inside my shirt.

Better idea: Don't wear it.

Must remember: I'm not Jewish. I can't wait for Christmas. I love bacon. Blend in. Be one of them.

"Libby!"

Dad's voice interrupts my list-making. He's somewhere downstairs, and I'm hunched over my desk, but his words boom out loud and clear. "Liberty Gordon!" Uh-oh. My full name. This will be an order. "We're starting our briefing. Your presence is requested. That's an order!"

"Yes, sir!" I shut my diary, scuttle out of my bedroom, then about-face back inside, take off my necklace, leave it on my desk, and then hurry back out. A briefing is what my parents call a family meeting. In our house, we speak English, Spanish, and Air Force. Pretty soon I'll know Greek.

Dad's wood-paneled office is empty. We've been here seven days, but I still don't know the routine of where we do things. "Where are you?" I shout into the vast space beyond his office, a living room called a *salon*, with crystal chandeliers and nine couches. Part of Dad's new job at the American embassy is throwing receptions with hundreds of people from around the world. That's why we need all the couches. Before this move, we lived in base housing where we had one couch and didn't need to shout to be heard. This room looks more like a fancy hotel than someone's house. It also makes me feel small, which I am for a twelve-year-old.

I wait for an answer. Silence. "Hello, where are you guys?"

"In the kitchen!" Mom calls. I follow her voice through the salon to the other side of the house, breathing in the smell of Pledge wood polish and flowers. This morning, I watched Melpo, one of our housekeepers, cut red roses and other flowers from bushes outside, then arrange them in silver vases. "*Loulouthia*," she said, pointing at them.

"Lou-lou-thea," I repeated.

"Bravo!"

Now I know *loulouthia* means flowers. My first Greek word.

When we moved in last week, Melpo was the first surprise. Our second and third surprises were Maria and Petros. Our new house comes with not one, but TWO women who clean every single day, PLUS a cook! No more chores for me! It's a dream come true.

Melpo, Maria, and Petros are new here like us, because the old staff quit their jobs when they found out we're Jewish. The Maratos family, who lived in the house before we came, told them they might not want to work for Jews, and they agreed. The new staff doesn't speak much English, but I can tell they don't mind we're Jews. It's like when people at a new school find out I'm Jewish and are suddenly mean and stop being my friend, but then I find people I like better. That happens sometimes.

Other times, I don't find people.

My parents and Justice are sitting at the kitchen table waiting for me. Mom and Dad exchange a glance, then flick their eyes back to me. Am I in trouble? I stay in the doorway. My sister, Justice, gets in trouble, not me. "Sorry I'm late."

Justice puts down her book, *Europe on Ten Dollars a Day*. She's leaving in two days to go backpacking through Europe with her friend Vonna before they start college in the spring. "The first order of business is that you're not sticking me with KP duty again, 'kay, Libby? It was your turn tonight."

"I'm sorry," I say, apologizing for the second time. "I thought we didn't have kitchen police duty anymore. We have Maria and Melpo for dishes and stuff."

Dad pulls his tie loose. "Now, hold on." He's not in his Air Force uniform. He wears suits for the embassy job now. It's so weird. "You still have chores."

"Absolutely," Mom agrees. "You still have chores."

"What? Why?" I can't believe this.

"Chores build character," Dad says. Whatever that means. Great. Now I'll have KP duty every night with Justice gone.

"Can we get on with this?" Justice asks. "I have to call Vonna about our itinerary."

"And I have my first day of school tomorrow, in case you forgot," I add.

"*Paciencia*," Mom says. Patience. One of her favorite words. "Libby, *kathiste*." I stare at her. "That means 'sit down' in Greek." She clasps her hands together. "We have fantastic news. You'll be very happy about it. Very."

I sit.

"Where's your necklace?" Justice suddenly asks me. "The one Grandma gave you for your birthday, with the Star of Dav—?"

"Can you stop interrupting? Mom was about to say something."

"Where is it?" she presses.

"I took it off."

"Why?"

"To clean it," I lie.

"Really?" She pokes her tongue in her cheek, which, with Justice, always means *I don't believe you*.

I point my chin at her. "Really."

"So, uh, how do you clean it? You've never cleaned your jewelry before. Just curious."

"I'll show you later."

"Yeah, I want you to."

"I thought you wanted to get on with this briefing." I turn away from her and angle my body toward Mom. "What's the big news?

Am I getting guitar lessons?" I wanted them for my birthday, but Mom said I had to take piano instead because girls shouldn't sit with their legs open when they play an instrument.

Dad leans toward me. "Something much better." He waits a couple seconds, then breaks into a huge grin. "You're going to get that Bat Mitzvah after all."

"What?" Clearly, I didn't hear him right. "Whose Bat Mitzvah?"

"Yours!" Mom practically screams. Then she starts talking at warp speed. Some people would have a hard time catching every word with her Cuban accent going so fast, but I'm used to it. "I know we said we would wait until you're older to have it in Israel like we did with your sister, but we can do it here. A Bat Mitzvah in Greece! *Imaginate?*" Her smile is a beaming crescent of joy. "Can you imagine that?"

No, I can't. I also can't talk. I shake my head. Words don't come. This cannot be happening.

"Look how surprised she is," Dad says to Mom.

"A Bat Mitzvah in Greece," says Justice. "That's going to be rad, Libs. Hey, can I invite Vonna?"

"Invite whoever you want," Dad answers. "You too, Libby. I'm sure you'll make a lot of new friends at school." The fact that he's so sure I'll have "a lot" of new friends shows how little he's aware of what school is like for me. I've hidden it from him, from both my parents. They think I'm as perfect and popular as Justice, that I'm some kind of younger version of my sister with a quieter personality.

But Justice knows. Her eyes meet mine. I look away.

"Who has a Bat Mitzvah in Greece?" Mom asks. "Lucky you, Libby."

Lucky? This is the worst thing that could possibly happen.

My face is frozen. I don't want a Bat Mitzvah. I've never wanted a Bat Mitzvah. I don't want people knowing I'm Jewish. WHAT ARE THEY TALKING ABOUT?!

The skin on my face is tingling. "How? I don't get it."

Mom grabs Dad's hand at the table and squeezes it. "You tell her."

Dad lets go of her hand and scoots his chair closer to mine. "Well, I checked with the base chaplain and he says we can use the chapel if we find a rabbi, because, you know, they won't send us one since it's not the High Holidays and there won't be enough Jewish personnel and all that."

"Well, if there's no rabbi, then there's no Bat Mitzvah," I say. There. Done. Thank G-d. "I mean, thank you for looking into it and everything, but I'll just have mine in Israel like Justice did. I think I would rather do that." *Without anyone knowing about it.*

Dad continues as if he hasn't heard me. "Then we realized, wait a minute, what about your cousin Josh? He just became a rabbi, and we can fly him in from Miami to tutor you and run the service. And get this—he has a Torah that he can bring on the plane. Pretty neat, huh? He'll stay here while you're learning your Torah portion. It's perfect."

"Perfect!" Mom echoes.

Josh? My cousin with the pimples and Star Wars cup collection from McDonald's who taught me how to burp the alphabet IS A RABBI NOW?

"I thought Josh was in film school," Justice says, as if this is a normal conversation.

Mom waves her hand like she's swatting a fly. "That was a phase. He was obsessed with that crazy shark movie, *Jaws*. Anyway, he's a fantastic rabbi now."

"I really think I should just wait and have it in Israel."

They don't hear me.

"Josh said early November would be good," Dad says. "We'll set the date this week. He can start teaching you over the phone."

"You'll have to start dress shopping now, Libs," Justice says. "In case you need alterations. Get something blue to match your eyes."

Mom talks about doing the reception at the house in the room with nine couches and how she can't wait for my relatives to come and hear how well I can sing. "When I was a girl in Cuba, I dreamed of having a Bat Mitzvah. But for girls, forget it. Impossible. And now my daughters…" She chokes up. "I wish my mother were alive to see this."

I stand up so fast, my chair crashes to the floor.

"I am not having a Bat Mitzvah." The words come out softly. "Ever. No Bat Mitzvah." My quiet voice scares them. I can see it in their faces. "I mean it."

I escape to my room but don't slam the door because slamming doors isn't allowed. I lie on my bed. My pillow is as warm as my tears.

Downstairs, I can hear murmurs and low voices, but Dad doesn't order me to come back. Neither does Mom. Then, there's a soft knock on my door.

"Permission to enter?" It's Justice.

"Permission granted."

She sits at my desk and looks at the piles of clothes all over my floor. "Wow, good luck getting your allowance because you're going to fail room inspection. What a sty."

"I was trying on outfits for tomorrow. Besides, I don't have to put any of this away. Melpo or Maria will do it."

"What's gotten into you? Talking back like that. That's not like you."

"What do you care? You're leaving." I stifle a sob. "Just go, since you're going anyway."

My face stays hidden in the safety of my damp pillow. I know she won't get out of my room until I come up with an answer. "I can barely read Hebrew. Plus, it's too much extra work. Seventh grade is going to be harder than sixth."

"Right. You're not a good liar, you know. I know what you're doing."

I lift my head up. She's holding my Star of David necklace above her head, swinging it back and forth. "Cleaning it, huh?"

I shrug.

"You think you're going to hide it? Losing battle. Big mistake. Huge."

"Put it back."

"I'll wear it if you don't."

"Don't you dare. Grandma gave that to me."

She tosses it to me. It lands next to my pillow.

"What do you think Grandma would think of you, ashamed of being Jewish?"

"I'm not ashamed."

"No? Then what would you call it?"

"None of your business. That's what I'd call it."

Justice paces back and forth in front of my bed. "You don't get it, Libs."

"You're the one who doesn't get it." A memory from last year in Virginia flashes through my mind. *You never said you were Jewish. You never told me. You never said.*

"It's simple. If you're confident about who you are, no one will mess with you. Trust me."

It's so easy for her to say that. Justice is eighteen, on the beautiful side of pretty, and fearless. She's everything I'm not. We've always stuck together for the first few weeks in a new post. This time I'll be on my own. She can't help me. *I'm not brave like you, Justice. I want to be, but I'm not. That's the problem. Trust me.*

She sits next to me. "I'd have given anything for a Bat Mitzvah where I could invite friends, especially if I could sing like you. I mean, sure, a Bat Mitzvah in Israel was special, but it was just you, me, Mom, and Dad at a restaurant afterward. You're getting the whole thing, the service, the party, the big occasion."

Something uncoils inside me, a tightness unwinding, an invisible

Ace bandage coming loose. "You remember what happened last year." My voice cracks, and I start to cry again. I can't help it.

She lies down, her head next to mine. Justice knows silence comforts me more than words. My sister can say a lot with just a look. She gives me one now and wipes a tear off my face with her sleeve. "Sure, I remember what happened," Justice whispers. "But that doesn't mean it'll happen again. It was a long time ago."

"Not that long."

It's been almost a full year now since Emily, my neighbor, ruined my life. She was at my house on a Friday after school. We'd been stationed in Virginia for three months, and Emily came over to watch TV. I was glad to have a friend in the neighborhood. She and I were eating giant bags of pretzels, even though it was almost dinnertime. From the family room, Emily and I could see Mom set out Shabbat candles in our tall, silver candlesticks, then take out our Siddur, the prayer book we use for Brachot, Friday night blessings. The book has a silver cover with turquoise stones surrounding Hebrew letters and was a wedding gift from my grandparents. My parents treat it like a treasure. Emily was watching Mom instead of the TV, especially when Mom accidentally dropped the Siddur, picked it up, and kissed it before putting it on the dining room table.

That's when Emily looked at Mom like she'd seen an alien. Emily asked me what Mom was doing.

"She's getting ready to light Shabbat candles. We're Jewish."

Emily's head jerked back as if I'd spit in her face or even slapped her. Her eyes darted around my house with new awareness, taking in the painting of the rabbi, the menorah on the shelf. "So you have to light those candles and talk in that language?"

"Yeah, it's Hebrew. Just on Friday nights. They're prayers, like, blessings, for the Sabbath. We call it Shabbat." She looked scared. And there was something else, something I couldn't figure out. "That's all. Then we have a nice dinner." I realized in that moment that this was going wrong, like maybe I wasn't explaining it right. When we were stationed in Texas, I'd lost a couple of friends who didn't like that I was Jewish, but they didn't have the expression Emily did. They'd just drifted away, and eventually, I found new friends and even another Jewish girl. With Emily, this felt different. Then it came to me. She was accusing me of something. But I didn't know what it was.

"Why did she kiss that silver book?" Emily demanded to know.

"Oh, that's just, if you drop a prayer book, you're supposed to kiss it."

Suddenly, she was in a rush to leave, grabbing her coat from a hook on the wall. Before bolting out the door, she kept repeating, "You never said you were Jewish. You never told me. You never said." After I closed the door, I watched her through the front window. She ran down the street toward her house as if she were being chased.

Then on Monday, Emily told everyone at the bus stop. Brad, the head bus bully, dropped loose coins in front of me when I stepped on the bus and told me to pick them up because "Jews are cheap."

No one let me sit next to them. That was the first day. The next day someone threw pennies at me. I didn't see who it was. I got Justice to drive me to school after that. The Jew attacks kept coming, steady, like waves in the ocean. Sometimes Emily would pretend-sneeze "a Jew" while her sidekicks, Tracy and Pam, echoed her. I can still hear their slicing laughs like dog bites. Emily never came over again. Neither did anyone else.

I ate lunch in the library. It was pointless to make new friends. The people in my chorus class seemed okay and probably wouldn't have minded if I'd eaten at their lunch table. But I wasn't interested in starting over. We were moving at the end of the school year. Seven months and I would be out.

Justice drove me to school for the rest of the year, even though I had to wake up earlier. I never told my parents. Maybe I should have, but I was worried they could have made it worse. I've thought of a thousand ways I could have lied to Emily that Friday night, told her my mother was an actress rehearsing a part with those Shabbat candles and prayer book, or maybe said Mom was a writer doing research for a book about Jews. I could have come up with pretty much anything other than the truth.

The truth will not happen this time. I pick up the necklace that Justice tossed on my bed and hide it in my hand.

✡ ✡ ✡

I get up extra early to blow-dry and curl my hair so my layers flip out like feathers on each side of my face like the women in *Charlie's Angels*. Then I read my prep list to remind myself of today's goals. I wear my new Levi's jeans from the BX, a blue top, and Justice's hoop earrings she let me borrow. I put my Star of David necklace in my desk drawer, all the way in the back. My purple backpack is filled with blank notebooks and sharpened pencils.

Mom and Dad take a quick picture of me, hug me, and leave for a meeting at the embassy. Petros makes a delicious tomato omelet for me, but I'm so nervous I only eat two bites. He takes two sesame seed bread rings called koulouria that he bakes every day, wraps them in wax paper, and puts them in my backpack. Maria and Melpo each kiss me on both cheeks before I walk out the door like they're my aunts.

I wait in front of our house for the bus. No other kids show up. I stare at a street sign with Greek letters next to a kiosk selling newspapers and candy, while a security guard hired by the embassy watches me. He stands in a booth yards away, part of our new life here. Small cars occasionally zip by. Then I see it. It's not a yellow school bus like the kind in the States. It's a green, hulking tour bus with a sign in the front window: *American International School of Athens.*

The doors open with a hiss, and I climb up the steps. Big kids stare back at me. Really big kids. I knew there would be high schoolers but didn't realize some would have beards and look older than my dad. Little kids are on the bus too, but not many people my age. The bus lurches forward and I hold on to the back of a seat, working my way in, looking for somewhere to sit. I feel like "a little ol' pinkie finger of a girl," a description the cafeteria lady in Virginia once gave me. Maybe Justice is so confident and finds friends easily because she's tall like my dad. I stand up straight, willing myself to have courage.

I spot an empty aisle seat with a backpack on it, next to a boy about my age who is sitting in the window seat.

I take a deep breath. "Excuse me, is anyone sitting—"

"No, please, go ahead." He takes the backpack off. He has a slight foreign accent and a friendly, open face. I plop down. Since the seat is covered in velvety fabric, it doesn't make that *pffft* farty noise like vinyl seats do on buses in the States. What a relief. I would have been thinking about that farty noise for the entire ride if that had happened.

Introduce yourself. I force myself to make eye contact. "Hi, I'm Liberty. Everyone calls me Libby."

"I'm Mohammed, but everyone calls me Mo. Nice backpack."

"Thanks."

"You usually don't see girls with backpacks at AISA. Only boys."

I side-eye a group of high school girls next to us. He's right. Colorful nylon purses and stacks of notebooks sit in their laps. I guess I'll leave my backpack at home. Every school has a custom or style that you don't find out about until after the first day.

I'm about to ask Mo if he likes AISA, when he says, "So you're in the Maratoses' old house. Your parents must be with the American embassy." It's not a question.

"My dad. How did you know?"

"This whole neighborhood is embassy people. This is what I'll tell you. Word gets out when a family moves out and a new one comes in."

I want to ask him if he knew the Maratos family because they were pretty prejudiced, but instead I ask, "Are your parents with the embassy too?"

"Not yours, the American one, no. My father works for the embassy of Turkey."

"Oh. Your English is really good."

"Thanks. It's probably because I haven't lived in Turkey since I was five. With so many American schools in foreign countries, I've had a very peripatetic existence, but my English has been consistent."

"Peri…what?" He laughs. So do I. "I have no idea what that means." I feel comfortable talking to him. Usually, I'm so nervous on first days that it's a struggle to push out complete sentences. It's not a stutter, more like a word flutter. But not this time. Mo is easy to talk to, even though he's obviously some kind of genius.

"Peripatetic means traveling from place to place. It's a good spelling bee word or SAT word."

"What grade are you in?" Maybe I'd made a mistake. Mo is probably small for his age, like me. I bet he's a senior in high school. He's being nice to me like some kind of babysitter. A heavy, sinking feeling lodges in my stomach.

"Seventh," he answers.

I feel lighter again. "Me too."

The bus suddenly screeches to a stop. Mo's backpack falls on the floor. He opens the window and leans out to see what's happened. "It's cats crossing the street. Athens has a cat overpopulation problem." He quickly takes an expensive-looking camera out of his backpack, points it through the open window, and snaps a few pictures. When the bus accelerates again, he puts the camera back. I notice a folder that fell out of his backpack, so I pick it up and hand it to him. He gives it back. "Take a look," he says.

I open it and find a stack of enlarged photos: street scenes of tourists at the Parthenon, close-ups of marble statues and their sculpted faces, stained glass windows of a church, old women with black headkerchiefs and craggy wrinkles, a crack in the sidewalk.

"What are these?" I want to know.

"I'm going to be a photographer someday."

"Wow, you took these?" He shows me more and we talk and talk. "I hope everyone at AISA is as friendly as you," I blurt. Right after the words escape, my cheeks flush. I'm probably as red as my mom's beet borscht.

But my compliment doesn't faze him. "I'll introduce you to some people. Not everyone at our school is friendly, but this is what I'll tell you. My friends are nice. At least you'll have somewhere to sit for lunch on the first day."

I like how he says "this is what I'll tell you" before making an important point.

It's a pretty long drive to school, and the bus winds and rolls through the hills of our neighborhood full of official diplomatic residences surrounded by high iron gates and security guard booths. We also pass several churches with beautiful windows and statues. There are so many churches in Athens, practically every few blocks. I don't see a single synagogue.

When we get off the bus, two girls and a boy are waiting for Mo. He introduces me to them: Sophia, Najla, and Henriq. They all say hi warmly. Sophia says she'll save me a seat at lunch.

I've never had such an easy first day in my life. Friends are falling into my lap.

I just have to make sure it stays this way. My hand flies up to my neck. Even though I know my necklace isn't there, I feel like I have to double check. This is a new beginning, another chance. I am not going to blow it.

The cafeteria is filled with the sounds of so many languages, it's like an international airport. At first, I don't see Mo and his friends. It's the Americans who are obvious right away, at a table near the front door, with their Nike sneakers and loud voices. One girl is wearing the same jeans I'm wearing from the BX, and her hair is carefully feathered like mine. She's obviously a military brat. The whole table probably is, with some embassy State Department students in the mix too. Last night, when I made my list, one of my goals was to make a friend at that table, but meeting Mo changed that.

I see him at a corner table. He gestures for me to come over, and I don't think twice about the American kids as I walk past them. Mo and his friends are eating souvlaki wraps with fries, so that's what I decide to get.

Sophia waits in the lunch line with me, and tells me she's Greek American, originally from Chicago, but she likes Greece better. She talks a whole lot. I like it because I don't have to think of things to say. She informs me that Najla is from France and Henriq is Swedish.

Guarantee you not one Jew in the bunch.

"Do they have any bacon?" I ask Sophia in the lunch line. "I love bacon."

"Um, no…I don't think so," she says. "That would be a weird thing to serve at lunchtime."

"Right. Of course. That would be totally weird." Mental note not to bring up bacon again. Maybe I shouldn't have put that on my prep list. It's not like Jews bring up bagels constantly.

Mo, Henriq, and Najla are all laughing when we sit down with our food trays.

"What's so funny?" Sophia asks.

Henriq pushes his long, blond hair out of his eyes and smiles at Sophia. "We all just think it's funny that Sophia means 'wisdom' and you showed up late to Mr. Macrides's class on the first day, no textbook, no pencil. Not too wise."

"Not wise in his class, especially," Najla says. "He's the strictest teacher and the hardest too."

Sophia looks up at the ceiling as if there's someone there. "Fine." She lowers her eyes and takes a big bite of her souvlaki wrap, talking with her mouth full. "Maybe my parents shouldn't have named me 'the wise one.' More like 'the stupid one.' In math, anyway. I'm definitely going to fail pre-algebra."

"I can tutor you," Mo says, dipping a french fry in ketchup. "Macrides doesn't scare me."

"What does your name mean, Najla?" I ask. She's pretty, with brown, wavy hair and high cheekbones.

"It means 'girl with big eyes.'"

We're all quiet for a second, and then we can't help but giggle.

"It sounds weird in English," Najla says. "My eyes aren't even that big, are they?"

"I guess our parents didn't know what to name us," I say. "My name is Liberty, and I have, like, no freedom. It's all rules in my house."

"Mine too," says Sophia. "Speaking of names, you all have to come to my name day party. September 17. Don't forget. You're coming, Libby, Liberty, whatever your name is. Big Eyes. Henriq. Mohammidy-mo."

"What's a name day?" I ask.

"I'm Greek Orthodox," she explains. "We celebrate the day on the calendar for the saint we're named after. It's like a birthday party with lots of food, but we dress up and there are adults there."

"Will there be champagne to toast you like last year?" Henriq asks.

"Yes, and wine and ouzo."

My jaw drops at this information.

"Greeks don't care about drinking age," Mo tells me. "You can have a glass."

My eyes widen. "Really?"

"Look, now who's the one with the big eyes?" Najla says, and everyone laughs.

"What's everyone doing for Christmas?" I ask, mentally checking off my prep list items.

"That's really far away," says Sophia. "Let's get through my name day first."

"Not all of us celebrate Christmas," says Mo.

You got that right, my new friend.

I've never had such a fantastic first day.

I'm at the sink washing dishes, humming. Mom instructed Maria, Melpo, and Petros to leave them there for me. I'll never escape KP duty, but I'm in such a great mood, I don't mind. Mom is near me, stirring a pot of rice on the stove. "You must have had a good first day of school." Even though Petros cooks for us, Mom still makes our favorites. "You sing when you're happy."

"I guess I am happy. I made a few friends. And I didn't get lost."

"That's fantastic. Tell me about your new friends."

"They're nice, from all these different countries."

"Who did you like the best?"

"Um...probably Mo. He introduced me and showed me around and stuff. This girl Sophia was nice. She invited me to her name day."

"Oh, a name day. She must be Greek. You can invite her to your Bat Mitzvah. Invite all your new friends. Mo too."

I stiffen at the sink but say nothing.

"Hey, how was it?" Justice asks, walking into the kitchen. She sits at the table. "How were your teachers?"

"Teacher-ish. They said teachery things, assigned us books and reading. Greek class was *polee kala*."

"What does *polee kala* mean?" Justice asks.

"Very good," Mom answers, sprinkling salt over the rice. "That's what it means."

"Did I hear you say something about the Bat Mitzvah?" Justice asks.

I turn around and shoot knives from my eyes. Why is she doing this, especially after the talk we had last night?

"The base chapel service will be just family," Mom says. "All the other guests will come and celebrate at the house. It's too many civilians to sponsor for base access. You know they're very strict because of terrorism threats and anti-Americanism these days."

I rinse off a few dishes, put them in the dishwasher. *Keep your voice casual, Libby.* "I told you, I'm not having a Bat Mitzvah." I turn and face Mom. "You can't force me."

Mom puts the lid on the rice pot and sits at the table next to Justice. "Come here." It's an order.

"Yes, ma'am." I dry my hands on the dish towel, then sit across from her and my sister.

"Do you know what a privilege it is to have a Bat Mitzvah?" she asks. "Even now, many synagogues don't allow a girl near a Torah, the religious ones."

"So maybe I'm turning religious."

Justice bursts out laughing.

"May I please be excused?" I ask, but don't wait for an answer. I stand up, push in my chair, go up to my room, and head straight out to my balcony.

Mom's voice follows me. "Listen, you are excused for now, but we are not finished with this conversation. We will talk about your Bat Mitzvah with your father here, believe me!" Then she shouts the same thing in Spanish to drive the point home.

Justice opens my door without knocking. She stands out on the balcony with me.

I speak without looking at her. "I didn't give you permission to enter."

"Vonna's going to be here any minute. We're leaving tomorrow and I need to talk some sense into you before I go."

I can see the columns of an ancient temple on a hilltop in the distance, a monument to some ancient god or goddess. The sun is going down, turning the marble a coral color. I read that networks of tunnels and caves lay underneath some of the ruins here. No one knows what they were used for. Even in ancient times, people had secrets. "I need you to be on my side with this," I tell Justice. "A Bat Mitzvah will ruin everything."

Justice leans on the balcony rail. "Hear me out. You know what I was thinking about today? When we used to go to Miami Beach with

Grandma and you'd insist on calling her 'Bubbe,' shouting, 'Bubbe, bring me my towel!' You told me you called her Bubbe in public because you wanted everyone to know you were Jewish. Remember?"

"So what? I was, like, five."

"You wanted the whole world to know. Because you were proud of us, of your family, of who you are. That's part of what a Bat Mitzvah is about, you know. You need to get in touch with that feeling you once had."

The balcony door swings open. It's Vonna. "Heeeeeey! Your mom told me to come on up." She drops her flowered suitcase with a thump. "Look at this view!"

"Heeeeeyyyy!" Justice answers in song, an inside joke they have. They squeal and hug and laugh for no reason. Then Vonna hugs me and swings me around. "Look at you, Libby. You've grown up since we were stationed in Texas. Seventh grade, wow!"

After all the greetings, we leave the balcony and go into my room. Vonna sits at my desk, crossing her legs. Justice and I lounge on my bed. I always love to see what Vonna is wearing. Today it's painter pants with a rainbow T-shirt and gold clogs. Her colorful bangles match the sparkling beads woven throughout her long, black braids. She has a ring on each of her fingers, even her thumbs. Vonna's planning to study art in college, and she already looks like an artist. "So!" she says. "I hear you're having a Bat Mitzvah."

I glare at Justice. "No, I'm not."

"Well, that's a shame. Because I was invited and would very much like to attend. My friend Rachel had one, and it was great. The party was, anyway. Rachel couldn't sing for the religious part. She sounded like a sick cat. You'd be a lot better because I *know* you've got pipes."

"Well, I'm *not having* one," I sing to her.

Vonna folds her arms. "Why not?"

Justice points her thumb at me like I'm not here. "She wants to pretend she's not Jewish so people won't be mean to her."

Vonna uncrosses her legs and leans forward. "Let me tell you something, Libby. Some people are going to be jerks to you no matter what. It might be because you're Jewish or it might be other things. I will always be Black and you'll always be Jewish and some people will always have a problem with that. But that's on them, you understand?" I nod. "You know what I think?"

I wait for her to tell me what she thinks. When Vonna talks, you can't help but listen. She has that way about her.

"Your Jewishness should be celebrated. My Blackness should be celebrated. Not swept under the rug. None of it. That never works anyway. Just makes things worse."

"That's what I've been trying to tell her!" Justice gestures toward the door. "C'mon, my mom made us rice and beans. She knows that's your favorite."

They clomp downstairs talking about their Europe trip, forgetting me. Dad comes home, and I hear all of them laughing and eating downstairs. I stay in my room, thinking. I'm not hungry. I sneak down later and fix a plate for myself, but only manage a few bites. Dad checks on me at bedtime and asks if I'm feeling well. I tell him I just have a lot on my mind.

I have a hard time falling asleep. I keep going over what Vonna and Justice said, what Mom said. Then I try to write in my diary, but I flip back a few pages and see this line I wrote a few days ago: Be seen and heard and let people get to know me.

Caring what my new friends think, people I barely know, seems so flimsy, so shallow.

Not everyone celebrates Christmas. Mo said it like it was no big deal.

Your Jewishness should be celebrated.

Do you know what a privilege it is to have a Bat Mitzvah?

I want to be brave. I want to be like Justice and like Vonna. Maybe it's easier when you're older.

Then again, it has to start somewhere.

Maybe it has to start with a Bat Mitzvah.

In the morning, there's a note from Justice on my desk. She left my Star of David necklace on top of it.

> Dear Libby,
>
> Vonna and I left at 5:00 a.m. and you were still sleeping, so I didn't wake you since I'll see you in a few weeks. I hope you think about everything we talked about. Please consider changing your mind. If you don't, it will be the first big fight you ever have with Mom and Dad, it will hurt them, and worst of all, you'll regret it forever. A Bat Mitzvah is a big deal. A milestone. You may not believe me, but you're going to feel different afterward. I promise you, you will. You'll feel more grown-up, more responsible and confident.

> Learning that haftarah and Torah portion is a great accomplishment, something to be proud of.
>
> You're worried about what your friends think about you. I understand that, but what if your new friends think it's an interesting, fun experience? Did you ever think of that? This isn't Virginia. The same thing is NOT guaranteed to happen again. Give these new kids a try. They might be happy to be included, like you were for that girl's name day. Too bad you can't read from the Torah on the Acropolis. That would be rad.
>
> Love you and see you soon,
>
> Justice

I read the letter five times.

Afterward, I put the necklace on. But I hide it inside my shirt.

At breakfast, Melpo points to the mezuzah we have nailed to the doorway, the decorative case that has scrolls inside with prayers. "What is?" she asks.

"Mezuzah," I answer. I point upward. "*Theos.*" I know that means "god."

"Me-zu-zah," Melpo repeats. "*Theos.*"

"Bravo!" I say.

Her kisses on my cheeks make me feel both loved and brave.

On the bus, Mo tells me about how Henriq is going to start a hockey team at AISA, but not enough kids know the sport. "He wants to teach me how to skate, but I don't think I'm athletic enough."

"But you'll try it?" I ask, only half listening. I can't stop thinking about my Bat Mitzvah situation, my lie, Justice's letter, everything.

Mo answers me while his eyes stay glued to the window, watching the scenery as we roll down a hill past gated houses. "This is what I'll tell you. If you don't try things, you'll never find out anything about yourself or anyone else. Besides, if I stink, I can always be the team photographer."

"Is there hockey in Turkey?"

"There is, yes, but I don't know anyone who plays."

"Turkey is a Muslim country, right?"

"Um, yeah, mainly. But there's also Christian and Jewish there. Why?"

"Nothing. Never mind." *Say it, Libby.* "Mo, um…"

"Yeah?"

"Have you ever wanted to, I don't know, not let people know you're Muslim?"

His head turns around, away from the view, eyes now focused on me. "My name is Mohammed."

I blink.

"It would be pretty hard to hide being Muslim with a name like Mohammed."

"Yeah, I guess so," I admit. We both crack up laughing. "Yup, that would be pretty stupid."

"You know what?"

"What?"

"I like being Muslim. I won the Koran competition last year at my mosque. I love our holidays and food. Eid is the best. And this is what I'll tell you. The truth matters. So, like, I would never want to hide my religion, my nationality, or anything about me."

Wow, what I would give to be so sure of myself. I wish I had the magic that Mo has, and Justice and Vonna. Now I'm the one who's looking out the window as we pass a church, kiosks, and a marble statue of a Greek soldier.

"Is there anything you want to tell me?" Mo asks. "Because I feel like you have something on your mind."

His face is open, trusting.

I want to tell Mo.

I really, really do.

I decide to borrow the expression he always uses. "This is what I'll tell you."

Yet the words won't come. I can't spit it out. I pull my necklace out. There it is. My Star of David. My secret. It rests on top of my shirt, over my heart.

"You're Jewish," he says. I nod. "My friend Daveed in Istanbul is Jewish too. We write to each other. He's having a Bar Mitzvah this year. Are you having one of those?"

I didn't cry once when those kids bullied me in Virginia. Not once. So why now? Why, when someone is kind to me, do I want to fall apart? How did I get so lucky to find a friend like Mo at my new school?

My eyes fill with tears, but Mo is nice enough to pretend it isn't happening. All he says is, "So, am I invited?" he asks.

I nod again.

"Do you need a photographer? My services are available."

I find my voice. "Yes, you're invited. Yes, you can take pictures, and yes, I'm inviting everybody!"

So, this is what bravery is. At lunch, I watch their faces for the change when I tell them, that subtle click behind the eyes, the rapid volley of looks back and forth that I expected. And it does happen. Sophia and Henriq have expressions that freeze for a few seconds, but then they go back to normal. "So," I explain, "you guys don't have to come to the service, but if you'd like to come to the party, it'll be fun with music and everything."

"I've never met a Jewish person before," Henriq says. "Will there be dancing in circles? That's all I know from movies. I'm sorry."

"There will be," I say. "They'll probably lift me on a chair too."

"Yes, I've seen that in movies, also," Henriq says.

"Will that scare you?" Najla asks. "I'm afraid of heights."

I'm more afraid of what people will think. "I'm afraid of heights too. Maybe I'll put a seat belt on the chair." Najla nods like that's a good idea. "Sooooo...will you guys come?"

Mo answers first. "Yes, and I'll take pictures. But I'm not dancing."

"I won't dance either," says Najla. "But I am very happy to come and thank you for inviting me. *Merci.*"

"Well, I'll dance," says Sophia. "All night long. But I can't tell my grandfather. He hates Jews. He blames Jews for everything bad in the world."

I suck in my breath. I feel sick.

I wait for someone to say something, but they keep eating like Sophia didn't just say something horrible.

"Yes, we know all about this grandfather," Mo says wearily. "I thought he blamed the Turks for everything bad."

"Them too," Sophia says, putting a straw in her Coke. "Wait, maybe he hates Americans more."

"Great, so you've got two marks against you, Libby," Najla says.

I can't breathe.

"What about Swedes?" asks Henriq.

Sophia slurps her Coke. "Hates them too, probably. I'll ask."

"But the Swedes gave us ABBA and meatballs!" Najla protests. "Is there anyone he likes?"

Sophia shakes her head. "Just Greeks. So I won't tell him I'm going to a Bat Mitzvah. And too bad you two aren't dancing. I love dancing!"

"Listen, we all have crazy relatives," says Henriq.

I feel my breath returning. Mo, Najla, and Henriq aren't too bothered by Sophia's grandfather or by my being Jewish. They aren't anything like the kids in Virginia either. Relief settles through me, steady and calming, and something else: a realization I've found friends. It's only been a couple of days, but I know this is what has happened. I reached the goal on my prep list. I found a friend on day one. More than one. More than I'd hoped for.

Because this is what I'll tell you: You can be yourself, and you don't have to hide anything. You can find friends who will see you, hear you, get to know you, and accept you for who you are. All of you.

"I definitely have crazy relatives," I admit. "You'll meet them at my Bat Mitzvah. My uncle Ben ends every occasion by playing the harmonica with his nose."

"I'll be taking a picture of that," Mo says. "Maybe even video."

"I'm really excited you guys are coming," I tell them. I can't believe how much I mean it.

"Coming to what?" I look up. It's one of the girls from the American table. I've seen her before. She sits next to me. "I'm Sonia. We're in English together. I noticed you were wearing the same jeans I have from the BX." She sort of waves at everybody, and they wave back. Sonia is freckly and smiley with big, feathered hair and braces. "I figured you must be American and new here. My table dared me to come over and say hi."

"Hi. I saw that too," I say. "About the jeans, I mean. I'm Libby."

"So what are you all talking about coming to?" she asks.

My hand flies up to my necklace. I adjust it to make sure it's still outside my shirt where everyone can see it.

"My Bat Mitzvah."

Pandemic Bat Mitzvah

Debra Green

1:37 a.m.

Go to sleep, Ruthie. Your Bat Mitzvah will be fine, I tell myself as I lie on my twin bed, with Schlepper (our chubby, black puggle-poo-hua-hua) snoring into my armpit. *You know all the prayers. Your speech is polished. You found the perfect dress for tomorrow.*

I pick up my phone from the nightstand and check the time. *Not tomorrow. Today! My Bat Mitzvah is today!*

1:58 a.m.

Nooo! I'm staring in the bathroom mirror, at the zit centered over my right eyebrow. It's brand new, pink, and monstrous.

Why did this happen to me? What did I do wrong?

It could be worse, I reassure my reflection. I could be one of the idol-worshipping Jews who had to spend forty years wandering the desert (the subject of my Torah reading).

I return to bed.

2:17 a.m.

Go to sleep, Ruthie. It'll be fine, I've been telling myself for the last thousand hours (or five).

But it won't be fine. I have a zit, one that will be memorialized for the rest of my life in every single Bat Mitzvah photo of me.

Also, there's a pandemic. A global pandemic!

We'll be outside. In good weather. With face masks and social distancing, I tell myself. *Your Bat Mitzvah will be fine. It's not forty years of wandering in the desert. It's just a few hours of sitting in the suburbs.*

Your Bat Mitzvah will be fine. It will be…

6:01 a.m.

I wake up suddenly. I don't want my Bat Mitzvah to be fine. Not *just* fine. I didn't go to Hebrew school all these years and work so hard on my prayers and speech so things could be fine. All my friends and family were supposed to watch me become a Bat Mitzvah. My relatives were going to fly in from Florida. I was going to have a party afterward almost as nice as my cousin Camilla's, with a buffet and dancing. My Bat Mitzvah was supposed to be amazing.

I whisper, "Stupid, awful (bad curse word here) pandemic!"

6:18 a.m.

Going back to sleep is completely impossible (or at least improbable). I get out of bed.

Schlepper follows me, and I let him outside to do his business. I do mine inside (and see that my zit has managed to grow even bigger), and we amble into the kitchen.

My brother (four years old and adorable) is sitting on the counter, wearing Big Bird pajamas and a Superman cape and eating a chunk of challah bread Mom baked yesterday.

He shoves his challah-holding hand behind his back. "Morning, Ruthie."

I grin. "Mom makes the best challah."

Leo grins backs, puts his hand out, and takes another bite.

"Let me help you off the counter. I don't want you to fall." I grab my brother by the waist and carry him down.

Then I tear off a big piece of challah for myself and a small piece for Schlepper, and I pour milk into cups for Leo and me.

The three of us sit on the couch, watching *Monsters, Inc.* for the eightieth time (or maybe eighth time). Snuggling with Leo and Schlepper, my favorite little monsters, soothes me. Maybe my Bat Mitzvah really will be fine.

8:00 a.m.

"Leo. Ruthie. Wake up," my mother, Ema, says.

I open my eyes.

Leo says, "Huh?"

Schlepper yaps.

My mother (coral lipstick, silky pantsuit, a big grin) is standing in front of us.

I yawn. "What time is it?"

"Eight o'clock," my other mother, Mom (wet hair, faded happy-face bathrobe, a big grin), says.

"Nooo!" I sit up straight. "Why didn't you wake us earlier?"

Mom kisses my forehead (the side opposite of the zit). "We wanted you to be rested for your big day."

"We have to leave for temple by eight thirty!" My voice sounds panicked. (That's because I'm panicked.)

"So don't potschke around. Get moving," Ema says. (She's an army drill sergeant. For real.)

"The bright side of the pandemic is there's less traffic, so it won't take long to get to temple," Mom says. (She's a paralegal. But she reads positive-thinking books like it's her job.)

I rush to the shower, almost too worried about getting ready for temple on time to worry about what will happen once I get there.

Almost.

8:45 a.m.

As we finally settle into Old Reliable (our ten-year-old Honda Accord), Leo whines, "Boogers are stuck up in my nose and it hurts and I hate this *owfit*." Oh, the inhumanity of a stuffed nose and a sweet suit and even sweeter polka-dot bow tie.

"You think *you* have it bad." I pat his cute head and try to ignore the finger crammed up his nose. "We're already late, a gigantic zit is hanging over my eyebrow, and I'm becoming a Bat Mitzvah during a pandemic."

"We still have plenty of time," Mom says from the front passenger seat. "And think of a pandemic Bat Mitzvah as an adventure."

"What about my zit?" I ask.

Mom turns and gazes at me. I know she's going to say no one will notice the zit or it's a good luck sign or some other positive-thinking phrase.

She opens her mouth, closes it, and looks away.

9:02 a.m.

As we near the synagogue, Mom says, "I know you'll do wonderfully today, Ruthie."

I shake my head a little. "You and Ema always say that. You'd tell me I'd do wonderfully if I were on my way to a Lakers tryout."

"You could be the first Jewish girl to make the team," Mom says.

"I'm four feet eleven."

"You'd make a good point guard," she says.

"Ruthie, I've heard you practicing the last few months," Ema says. "You chant all the prayers beautifully, and you worked hard on your speech."

"And your dress is gorgeous," Mom adds.

"Thanks," I say. It's not a designer gown like my cousin Camilla wore to her Bat Mitzvah, but it's delicate and lacy and I like it a lot.

"I can't get my boogers out," Leo says.

"Stop picking your nose," I tell him.

"Look on the bright side. Leo can't pick his nose once he puts his mask on," Mom says.

I frown (looking on the gloomy side). "I never thought I'd have a masked Bat Mitzvah."

"Your pandemic Bat Mitzvah will be unique," Mom chirps.

But I don't want a unique Bat Mitzvah. I want what I was supposed to have: a lunch reception at the Holiday Inn, with a DJ and seventy-five guests. I never even asked for what Camilla had: a dinner party with a fancy band on a huge yacht. She had a salad bar, taco bar, nacho bar, baked potato bar, soda bar, chocolate bar, and a regular bar for the adults. That's the Bat Mitzvah gold standard, which I know we can't afford. But I never thought my service and reception would be held outside in the temple parking lot with only twenty masked guests spaced six feet apart.

I think about the wandering Jews in my Torah reading, tell myself I'm a lot better off than them, remind myself that a Bat Mitzvah is supposed to be about the Torah and prayer and G-d. (I'm not completely convinced.)

Ema pulls into the lot. She says, "We need to organize everything fast. We have to clear out of here by thirteen hundred hours for the next Bat Mitzvah." (Our synagogue used to hold Bar and

Bat Mitzvahs for two kids at a time. Now, to avoid crowds, there's one Bat Mitzvah at ten a.m. and a second one at one p.m. Another "unique" gift from the pandemic.)

"Here we are!" Mom says. "Beginning Ruthie's perfect Bat Mitzvah day!"

"Got it!" Leo shouts. He holds up his finger. There's a huge ball of bloody boogers on it.

Ema swerves the car into a parking space.

Leo's finger jabs into my chest, splattering bloody boogers onto my white lace dress.

Perfect.

9:04 a.m.

I rush out of the car and into the synagogue bathroom. I scrub the front of my bloody dress with soap and water. The small red drip turns into a large pink blob.

I use paper towels to blot my dress as dry as possible (not very), then walk out to join my family.

Mom and Ema are wearing identical homemade face masks that say *Proud Mother*. Ema is cleaning Leo's hand with a disposable wipe. He has on a *Proud Brother* mask.

Mom hands me a homemade pastel pink mask that spells out *Bat Mitzvah Girl* in dark pink glitter. She says, "On the bright side, your mask now matches your dress."

And my zit.

Ema points to the area where I'll become a Bat Mitzvah. "What do you think of our handiwork?"

"It's really nice," I say (truthfully). About ten large canvas umbrellas, their tall stands vined with red roses, tower above a sprinkling of padded folding chairs. Bright green bedsheets cover the asphalt to resemble grass (but really look like sheets). Morty, the synagogue's security guard, stands by a wooden TV console posing as an ark. Next to the fake ark is a podium and chairs for the rabbi, the cantor, and (gulp) me.

"You'd hardly know this is a parking lot," Mom says.

I nod. But I totally know this is a parking lot. Everyone will know this is a parking lot. And it's nothing like the beautiful yacht with twinkle lights and thick red carpeting that Camilla's family rented for her Bat Mitzvah.

My uncle David walks over, holding a camera and wearing a kippah and the *Official Photographer* mask Mom made for him.

He's not really a photographer. (He manages a discount shoe store.) But he owns a fancy camera, and he took a photography class at the community college last year. We didn't want to waste one of our twenty guest slots on a professional we didn't know. So he's our photographer today.

"Ruthie, you look pretty as a picture." Uncle David holds up his camera. "Get it? Picture?"

I humor him with a laugh. What's really funny is posing for pictures with a monstrous zit on my forehead and a weird pink blob on my chest. (Terribly, terribly funny.)

My mothers, Leo, and I take off our masks for the pictures.

"My nose is bursting," Leo announces.

"It's not," Uncle David says. "Get it? It snot."

Leo doubles over with laughter. "Snot! Snot, snot, snot!"

I'm both thirty years too young and nine years too old for the joke. I sigh.

"We need to get moving," Ema says.

Uncle David raises his camera, then puts it down. "Ruthie, there's something over your eyebrow."

"It's a zit," I say.

He frowns. "Oh." Then he smiles. "Pore you. Get it? P-O-R-E."

No one laughs.

"Please just take the pictures," I say as politely as I can. (But I hear the irritation in my voice.)

Uncle David nods. "A little Photoshop and you'll have a smooth complexion. I don't know about the schmutz on your dress though."

I sigh again. "We're meeting with Rabbi Levinson at nine fifteen. That's, like, a minute away."

"Nine fifteen is Jewish time for *nine thirty-ish*," Mom says. "We're not a prompt people, culturally speaking. So don't worry about the rabbi showing up just yet."

Rabbi Levinson shows up.

9:25 a.m.

I stand in the back of the parking lot with Rabbi Levinson and

Cantor Ellis and my closest friends and family members who we've given the honor of aliyahs (blessing my Torah reading).

"We're thrilled that Ruthie has chosen to become a Bat Mitzvah," the rabbi says. "We know she'll do a great job leading the service today."

He starts to say something else, but his words are drowned out by a motorcycle roaring down the street behind us. He stops and waits. When it's (relatively) quiet again, he says, "The *setting* where you become a Bat Mitzvah is unimportant. Once you know how to read the Torah and chant the Hebrew prayers, you can lead a service anywhere. Our people have held services in all kinds of places—hidden caves during the Spanish Inquisition, Ethiopian farmland, lavish synagogues in Beverly Hills, or this simple parking lot. We Jews always find a way to form a community, gather together, and pray."

I nod. I'm proud to be carrying this tradition forward. But I still wish our community today weren't limited to twenty people and we didn't have to gather in a parking lot.

"Now who's familiar with aliyahs?" the rabbi asks.

"We are!" my aunt Rachel says. She and my uncle Mark and cousin Camilla are aliyah pros, because Camilla became a Bat Mitzvah right before the pandemic. My cousin looks like a princess today, in a beautiful, sparkly turquoise dress with a full tulle skirt, like a longer version of a ballerina's tutu. (And *her* dress isn't stained.)

Cantor Ellis talks to them for a couple of minutes, then moves on to my grandma Judy, who takes much longer to understand her aliyah. She's hard of hearing and can't read the cantor's lips under her mask.

Meanwhile, our neighbor, Mrs. Nossaman, asks a ton of questions. ("Rabbi, when is it my turn? Cantor, where should I stand? Ruthie, what happened to your dress?")

Mom keeps saying (shouting, really, due to Grandma Judy's hearing problem), "You'll do great!" and "You got this!"

"My nose hurts," my brother whines.

"You're fine," Ema soothes, her eyes on the rabbi.

I look over at Leo. He's not at all fine! Blood is dripping from his mask, down his chin, onto his suit, and onto the green bedsheet over the parking lot.

"Leo's bleeding!" I yell.

He starts crying and hurls himself into my arms, and I hug him tight.

Morty runs toward us, looking fierce and carrying something that looks like a metal baton.

My mothers rush over. Ema gets to us first (army conditioning), takes Leo from me, and says, "It's all right, kids. It's just a nosebleed."

I exhale relief.

"I'll get the first aid kit," Morty says, running toward the synagogue.

"Use this for now." Mrs. Nossaman retrieves a pack of tissues from her purse and throws them at us.

Mom stuffs a tissue up Leo's nose and uses the rest to gently blot the blood from his chin and neck.

Uncle David says, "I take it you don't want a picture of this?"

I look down. Blood is splotched over my dress, my legs, my shoes. The green sheet over the asphalt is speckled with red drops, like a weird Christmas decoration. (Wrong decor for a Bat Mitzvah.)

I glance at my brother. He seems calm now, sucking on a lollipop (also from Mrs. Nossaman's purse).

I'm not at all calm. "Leo," I say, "I told you not to pick your nose. You made a huge mess!"

"Ruthie." Ema's voice is sharp. "Have some compassion."

Mom says, "You'll laugh about this one day."

I glare at her and speak slowly, shaking my head with every word: "I will never. Ever. Ever laugh about this."

"We'll have to delay the Bat Mitzvah," Rabbi Levinson says.

"Not too long though," Cantor Ellis says. "We're already running late, and at one o'clock we need to start preparing for Journey Markowitz's Bat Mitzvah."

I point to my brother and yell, "Look at what you did, Leo! You totally ruined the most important day of my life!"

Leo bursts into tears.

For the second time this morning, I run to the bathroom.

9:39 a.m.

I stand at the sink, splashing water on my arms and dress. I'll get to my legs next, and then the shoe spatters. I'll wipe the tears off my face if I can ever manage to stop crying.

I try to cheer myself up. I tell myself: *At least I don't have to wander the desert for forty years.*

I do not cheer up. I picture Moses guiding the wandering Jews and G-d sending them manna bread from the sky. They didn't have it so bad. As far as I know, none of the wandering Jews spent their Bat Mitzvah day with their brother's gross nosebleed all over them. They worshipped a golden calf, but G-d showed them mercy and helped them find their way. It's all in this morning's Torah reading (if there will even be time for this morning's Torah reading).

I quietly chant my Torah portion while I scrub my dress with a soapy paper towel. The chanting soothes me. (My scrubbing, however, doesn't do much good.) I stop crying.

I think about my wandering Jewish ancestors. After they prayed to G-d with all their hearts and souls, He led them out of the desert.

I turn off the faucet, set down the wet paper towel, close my eyes, and whisper with all my heart and soul, "G-d, please help me. I want to become a Bat Mitzvah today, to commit to Judaism, to make my family and friends proud, to make You proud."

There's a knock on the bathroom door.

I open my eyes wide, stare at the door, and whisper, "G-d?"

9:49 a.m.

Camilla walks in.

Of course it's not G-d. (For one thing, He doesn't need to knock.) He's already here.

Still, I can't help sighing. I tell Camilla, "Use the portables outside. This bathroom's too small for social distancing."

"I'll try to keep some space between us," she says. "But I should be immune to COVID-19."

"Oh." I nod slowly. "Right." The word comes out in a whisper. Camilla and her parents had the virus in April. Her dad (my uncle Mark) was hospitalized for three scary days.

"Are you OK?" she asks.

"Terrific," I say (sounding the opposite of terrific). As I gaze at my cousin in her sparkly princess/ballerina dress and matching sparkly face mask (snot free, blood free), I stop feeling so sorry for her. "You can't pee in a portable?"

"I came to check on you, Ruthie." She grabs some paper towels from the dispenser and gets them wet. "I know how nerve-wracking Bat Mitzvahs are. I just had mine a few months ago, remember?"

"I remember. Your one hundred and fifty guests. The yacht. The ten-piece band."

"Five-piece band, not ten. Five was more than enough." She bends down low and starts cleaning the blood off my shoes.

"And all those bars," I say.

"Yeah. So many people got drunk. I heard Uncle Jeremy passed out."

"Not just the *bar* bar. The taco bar. The potato bar. The chocolate bar."

"I didn't even eat that night," Camilla mutters. She stands and tosses the wet paper towels into the trash. "How can I help?"

I look down at my shoes. No splatters in sight. "Thank you for that," I say. "There aren't any more ways to help. The bloodstains won't come off my dress."

Camilla looks me up and down. Then she says, "Wear mine."

I stare at her.

She nods. "We're about the same size."

(I'm a little shorter and scrawnier.) "But what would *you* wear?" I ask.

She points to my dress.

My jaw drops.

"You're my cousin and I love you," Camilla says. "But I'm not spending your Bat Mitzvah day in my bra and underwear."

"You love me enough to spend the day in my wet dress stained with Leo's nose blood?" A tear falls down my cheek.

Camilla smiles. Her eyes are wet too. She reaches over her shoulder for her zipper.

Another knock. "Ruthie, are you all right?" Mom asks.

"Much better now," I call out, returning Camilla's smile. "How's Leo?"

"Much better too. We stopped the bleeding. He's putting on the spare clothes we keep in the car."

"Did you happen to see any of my clothes in there?" I ask.

"Sorry, Ruthie. There's no spare Bat Mitzvah dress."

I smile wider and whisper to Camilla, "Yes, there is."

"I need the spare clothes, Aunt Lucy," Camilla says loudly.

"Camilla?" Mom asks.

"Long story," she says. "Can you find something that sort of fits?"

Silence. Then Mom says, "I'll see what I can do."

9:58 a.m.

Camilla's dress looks beautiful on me and fits well, once we stuff the bodice with toilet paper. As I smooth out the toilet paper, Camilla says, "Now you've become a woman."

We giggle.

"I can't believe you're doing this for me," I say.

"Believe it. I feel bad you got stuck with a pandemic Bat Mitzvah."

"Yeah." I frown. "It wouldn't have been as fantastic as yours, but—"

"My Bat Mitzvah wasn't so fantastic," Camilla says. "Remember I had to share it with Adriana Weiner?"

I nod (even though I'd forgotten).

"Do you know she's been taking opera classes since she was ten? I sounded like a drowning mouse compared to her."

"No, you didn't," I say. (More like a dying bird.)

"And then that stupid party boat."

"I loved the boat!"

"You didn't get seasick." Camilla frowns. "I started retching as soon as they pulled up the anchor. And that obnoxious bandleader kept shouting at people to get the Bat Mitzvah girl on the dance floor. Except he got my name wrong. He kept calling me Amelia. I just wanted to lie down and barf into the ocean."

I'd been completely wrong about Camilla's Bat Mitzvah. I'd

worshipped it like the wandering Jews had worshipped the golden calf. But the yacht, the band, the dancing—they were all false idols.

10:07 a.m.

Ema walks into the bathroom with a tote bag. "Mom told me about your girls' predicament," she says. "We asked around. This is all we got on short notice." She hands Camilla the bag. "Ruthie's gym clothes were in the car. Your grandmother gave us the sweater she's knitting. Morty gifted us with his sweatshirt, and your uncle David donated a cardigan."

"Thank you!" Camilla enthuses as if Ema has brought new designer dresses.

"Thank *you*, Camilla," Ema says. "And, wow, Ruthie, you look beautiful. That dress fits you per—" She stares at my stuffed chest and raises her eyebrows. Then she clears her throat and says, "Don't take too long mulling over these glorious fashion choices. Journey Markowitz will be claiming the parking lot at thirteen hundred hours." (Army talk for 1:00 p.m.) Ema glances at my chest again, shakes her head, and walks out.

We go through the merchandise. Grandma's sweater will be pretty when it's done, but the unfinished neckline looks like it could unravel with one yank of the yarn, and there aren't any sleeves yet. Morty's sweatshirt is huge and says "Number 1 Dad" on it.

Camilla tries on my gym clothes, a polyester T-shirt and shorts in forest green and dark brown (the colors of Louella M. Nelson

Middle School). Thankfully, they're clean. The shorts fit, but the top is very tight. Camilla shrugs and covers the outfit with Uncle David's gray cardigan, which comes down almost to her knees.

"Gorgeous," I joke.

Camilla smiles. "Keeping it classy."

We leave the bathroom together, six feet apart but extremely close.

10:18 a.m.

My brother sits cross-legged on the asphalt of the parking lot, watching Ema, Aunt Rachel, and Uncle Mark use disposable wipes to clean the blood from the green bedsheet. Leo is wearing his Batman pajamas and a disposable white face mask with *Proud Brother* scribbled on it with a thick black marker. He has no reason to be proud of me today.

I rush over, crouch down in front of him, and say, "I'm so sorry, Leo!"

He frowns. "I ruined your *Bah Missbah*."

I shake my head. "You didn't. Not at all. I never should have said that."

He stares up at me with his big brown eyes. (I notice a spot of blood on his chin.) He says, "I shouldn't have picked my nose."

"It's OK." I hug him. "I'm sure you learned a lesson."

He nods. Then he puts his finger in his ear and digs around.

Our mothers walk over. Mom says in a choked voice, "You look wonderful, Ruthie."

Ema reaches for Mom's hand. "Oy vey. The Bat Mitzvah hasn't

even started, and you're already tearing up." (Ema sounds as choked up as Mom.) "Ruthie, I'm so proud of you."

"How do you make a mouse smile?" Uncle David asks. Before anyone can answer, he says, "Say cheese." Then he laughs at his own joke and clicks the camera. He's finally gotten a picture of us. (Hopefully my fake chest will distract from my real zit.)

10:26 a.m.

Rabbi Levinson, Cantor Ellis, and I sit on the makeshift bimah and wait for everyone to take their socially distanced seats.

Six feet in front of me, Mom smiles wide and flashes me a thumbs-up sign. Leo looks adorable, though he's digging in his ear again. Ema uses her drill sergeant voice to demand everyone get seated before ten thirty. My people. Under the toilet paper padding my chest, I feel my heart swell.

I look at Camilla in the (let's face it, ugly) sweaterdress, next to her parents who still seem pale from their battles with COVID-19. I gaze at my grandmother, in a medical mask, plastic face shield, surgical gloves, and her fanciest dress. Then I look at Uncle David, with his big camera and his goofy grin, and Mrs. Nossaman, who's intently studying the paper with her aliyah on it, and my closest friends from temple and middle school, sitting six feet apart but likely texting each other. They've all dedicated part of their weekend to hearing me chant Hebrew in a parking lot. I'm so grateful for their love and support.

Maybe there's a bright side to wandering the desert for forty years. That's a long time to develop relationships. The wandering Jews may have been physically lost, but they found their community. And I found mine.

I close my eyes and imagine the Jews who've gone before me, whispering prayers in caves in Spain, chanting Hebrew on Ethiopian farms, reading from the Torah in Beverly Hills. I picture Camilla, leading the service in her synagogue a few months ago.

I think about the Jews who will come after me. Journey Markowitz in a few hours. My brother in nine years. I'll be so proud of him no matter where his Bar Mitzvah is held. (As long as he's stopped picking his nose by then.)

10:30 a.m.

Mom orders the last stragglers seated, beams at me, and sits herself down.

Rabbi Levinson leans over and murmurs, "Is everything fine, Ruthie? Are you ready to become a Bat Mitzvah?"

I nod. "Everything's fine. More than fine. It's perfect."

Bar Mitzvah on Planet Latke

Henry Herz

Multicolored lights flashed and music thumped at Noomin's Bar Mitzvah party. I shuffled along the edge of the plasteel dance floor, watching the other kids. Shayna-punim faced Noomin, her Denebian silk dress twirling gracefully, while he lurched from side to side in powderpuff blue six-legged tuxedo pants.

I've been friends with Shayna-punim since first grade. Not only did she have a pretty face with purple eyes and gorgeous fangs, but she was also smart and kindhearted (in all three hearts).

Kvetch sidled up to me, stuffing a fried lumpyworm into his beak. "Hey, Schlimazel. Noomin sure knows how to throw a party, huh?" he said, tilting his head toward the dance floor.

"Mmmm," I agreed, still watching Shayna-punim.

Kvetch smiled. "Why don't you ask her to dance?"

My pulse raced in panic at the thought. I was too shy to ask her to dance. "I'm not a good dancer. I've been told more than once that I'm all left tentacles."

The song finished and Shayna-punim strolled off the dance floor...toward me.

I changed my skin color to blend in better, retreating to the dessert bar before I could embarrass myself.

I shambled home after the party. My three parents were relaxing on the xenon-filled living room couch.

"How was the party, dear?" Mom asked.

"Fine," I replied without smiling.

Mom, Dad, and Nan exchanged a look. Nan stood, laying a tentacle lightly across where my shoulders would be, if I had shoulders. "Would you like some Betelgeuse Creme Pie?"

I shook my head. "No thanks, Nan." What I wanted was to be less shy around Shayna-punim.

* * *

The next morning at school, my history teacher pointed to an elderly silver-scaled guest. "Class, please welcome former astronaut and marine biologist, Dr. Nosh. I invited him to talk about the history of religion."

"Thank you, Ms. Maven," he replied with a nod. "I led the first science mission from Latke to Earth. We collected specimens and data about spirituality since we never developed our own religions. We subsequently adopted some Earth faiths.

"Can someone tell me what else we brought back from Earth?" he asked, eyes twinkling.

Shayna-punim's graceful tentacle shot up.

"Yes, miss."

"You also brought back ten species of saltwater fish."

"Correct. Latkenites have enjoyed smoked salmon and pickled herring ever since. What else?"

Desserts. I didn't say it because I was probably wrong.

"Cakes and pies and cookies," Noomin shouted.

"Very good," said Dr. Nosh. He patted Noomin on the back.

That darn Noomin!

Dr. Nosh continued, "Now, I visited Earth over a hundred years ago. How is that possible?"

Relativistic time dilation…probably.

Again Shayna-punim raised a tentacle. "Time dilation—the slowing of time from the perspective of a fast-moving traveler."

Dr. Nosh gave an approving nod. "Correct."

I told you she was smart. She smells nice too. *I'm such a klutz.*

After class, Kvetch shuffled with me to the cafeteria.

"What's with the faded, baggy pants, Schlimazel? Kinda sloppy."

The fact that he was right didn't help my mood. More grousing followed, so I tuned out his nonstop yada, yada, yada. I needed to figure out how to overcome my shyness toward Shayna-punim. *Noomin's party impressed her. Hmm. My Bar Mitzvah's coming up. Maybe I should throw a super fancy party.*

Aromas assaulted our nasal sacs when we entered the cafeteria. Today's special was squillian chowder.

"Ugh, I can't stand squillian," Kvetch confided a bit too loudly.

"Then, no soup for you," replied the stern-faced lunch lady.

Kvetch shrugged, which is not easy to do without shoulders. He bought a number five, roasted free-range hosenpud bird with fried tubers and a Fomalhaut fizz, before heading outside. I lost my appetite and sat by myself to brood about Shayna-punim.

Just because I throw a big party, that doesn't mean she'll come. And if she does come, she might not have a good time. And if she has a good time, it might be with someone else.

"Hi, I'm Meshuggener."

I looked up at a tall, smiling nemale. Latkenites have three biological genders: male, female, and nemale.

"This is my first day here, so I don't know anyone yet. Can I eat with you?" Meshuggener asked and pointed at a chair.

"Um, sure," I replied, extending a tentacle sucker side up. "I'm Schlimazel."

Meshuggener's tray held a steaming bowl of squillian chowder and a big piece of chocolate babka.

"I see you got the squillian," I said. "Brave."

Meshuggener grasped a spoon. "Sometimes squillian's good,

sometimes not. You never know unless you try, right?"

I admired the risk-taking attitude. It had taken me weeks to approach other kids when I first arrived here.

We compared schedules and discovered that Meshuggener would be in my math and history classes and had signed up for Earth English.

"English," I said, as I raised my antennae. "That's a tough class."

Meshuggener smiled. "I'll just have to work harder."

This kid is crazy.

Meshuggener glanced at the bare tabletop in front of me. "Have you eaten? I'll share my babka with you."

Nice. "Thanks. I'll go buy my usual—tuna on toast with…" I lost the power of speech as Shayna-punim approached.

"Hi, Schlimazel."

All I could do was grin and nod back.

"Hi, I'm Meshuggener. I'm new here."

She flashed that dazzling smile. "I'm Shayna-punim. Nice to meet you. See you both later," she added before sitting with some friends.

Amazing! Meshuggener had talked to her like it was the most natural thing in the world. *What I wouldn't give to do that.* I paused to consider what just happened. It became very clear to me that every decision I'd ever made, in my entire life, had been wrong. My life was the opposite of everything I wanted it to be. Every instinct I had, in every walk of life, be it something to wear, something to eat…had all been wrong. From now on, I would do the complete opposite, I vowed. "On second thought, I'm gonna try the squillian chowder."

I bought my lunch and returned to the table to find two females sitting with Meshuggener.

Meshuggener smiled and gestured. "This is Tchatchke, and this is Verklempt. They were looking for a table, so I invited them to join us."

Wow. My usual reaction to sharing a lunch table with strangers involved staring silently at my food.

"Hi," I managed. *Smooth.* I tasted my squillian chowder to mask my weak response.

"That's courageous," noted Tchatchke.

"It's good today," I replied, winking at Meshuggener. "You never know unless you try, right?"

When I finished my chowder, Meshuggener gave me half the babka.

The females split a sardine muffin. "The top's the best part," said Verklempt.

"They should only bake muffin tops," I suggested, embracing the new bolder me.

The others nodded in agreement. The females finished their dessert and rose. "Nice meeting you, Meshuggener and Schlimazel."

Verklempt remembered my name.

"Hey, do you wanna play catch after school?" I asked Meshuggener, surprising myself. "I've got a low-gravity dodecahedron in my locker."

Meshuggener gave me a tentacle bump. "Sounds good. See you then."

That afternoon, I did the opposite of what I usually do: I spoke to one new person in each of my classes.

✡ ✡ ✡

That week, I tried a new cafeteria food each day. Mostly, they tasted surprisingly good, although the hosenpud bird burgers smelled like poodoo. I even worked up the nerve to say hi to Shayna-punim. Once. She rewarded me with that beautiful smile. I nearly melted in my chair.

Meshuggener and I made a point to sit and eat lunch with other kids. We hung out after school and did math and history homework.

✡ ✡ ✡

I took my seat directly behind Shayna-punim in history class, with Meshugenner to my right. *Maybe I should sit in* front *of her.* But before I could move, Noomin plopped down. *Noomin!*

He turned in his chair. "Hey, Shayna-punim. Have you figured out yet what you're going to do for your mitzvah project?"

"Well..." she replied, curling a smooth tentacle to her face.

She's adorable.

"At first I was going to volunteer to work at an animal hospital," she continued. "But then I decided to collect toys for kids at the Glick Orphanage. Those poor kids have no moms, dads, or nans.

Can you imagine how difficult that must be for them?"

I knew she was kindhearted. I filed away the name of the orphanage. You never knew when something like that could come in handy.

Out of the corner of my eye, I noticed Meshuggener grinning at me.

Ms. Maven slid into the room, so I had to tear my attention away from Shayna-punim.

✱ ✱ ✱

It was a nice rainy day, so Meshuggener and I ate lunch outside.

Shayna-punim slid by with a friend, giggling.

My hearts fluttered.

"She has a cute giggle, doesn't she?" Meshuggener asked.

My face flushed blue.

Meshuggener laughed. "Ha. I *knew* it. You've *so* got a crush on her."

I felt like my old self again: totally inadequate, completely insecure. I sighed. "Yup. A big one."

"And?" Meshuggener replied, gently cuffing the side of my head. "What are you going to do about it?"

Hmm. Doing nothing about it hadn't worked. Maybe I should do the opposite. "Well, she's helping the Glick Orphanage. I could do my mitzvah project for them too. I bet she'd like that."

Meshuggener leaned closer. "Agreed. But what's a mitzvah project?"

I set down my sandwich. "So, a Bar Mitzvah is a Jewish religious ceremony to celebrate when a child becomes responsible for their own behavior, like an adult. The mitzvah project is something I have to do to help a charity. I also have to lead a Sabbath service."

Meshuggener's eyes widened. "That sounds like a lot of work. Good for you."

"After the service, there's usually a big party," I added, salivating at the thought of all the fish and desserts.

"Fun," replied Meshuggener. "Do you get to invite who you want?"

"Yes." I grinned. "Don't worry, you're definitely invited."

"Thanks. But that's not what I was thinking. You should invite Shayna-punim."

I said nothing. Raindrops pitter-pattered on the tabletop. My old fears rose. My throat tightened. *Even if I invite her, she might not accept. And if she accepts, I might embarrass myself. And if...* STOP. *Do the opposite.* I took a deep breath. "Yes. I will invite her." That felt good to say out loud.

Meshuggener smiled. "Now, how are you going to impress her?"

"You're relentless," I replied. "Well, there'll be lots of delicious food."

"Think bigger," Meshuggener urged.

"Um, I could have a DJ playing music."

"Good. What else?"

"Uh, the party table centerpieces could be toys," I said.

"Toys?"

"That I give to Shayna-punim after the party for the orphanage," I replied with a wink.

"Nice!"

"I could order holographic Bar Mitzvah invitations."

"Yes!"

"Monogrammed party favors."

"That's it. Keep going!"

"A 3-D printed icing image of my face on a cake!" I cried, caught up in Meshuggener's enthusiasm.

"Okay, reel it back. Too much." Meshuggener laughed. "But that's the spirit. Go strong or go wrong."

And just like that, there I sat, wearing a goofy grin, rain dripping from my chin.

✶ ✶ ✶

After school, I stopped by the Glick Orphanage to ask what they needed. My tentacle froze in midreach for the glassteel door handle. Shayna-punim stood with her back to the door, speaking with the receptionist. I slid behind a bush near the door and turned on the audio amplifier of my communicator device. Eavesdropping on my crush—not my proudest moment.

"Are there any specific types of toys the orphans like?" asked Shayna-punim.

"Well, dear," replied the receptionist, "any toys would be fine. But how soon can you provide them? You see, we have a fission reactor that generates our electricity. Unfortunately, even at minimal usage, we only have enough fuel left to last until the nineteenth of next month. We need at least two hundred kilograms of yellowcake uranium no later than 5:00 p.m. on the eighteenth so we have time to smelt new fuel rods."

My Bar Mitzvah's on the eighteenth, I thought.

"Oh no," replied Shayna-punim. "What will happen if you don't get the fuel by then?"

"We'd have no electricity to run our climate and atmospheric regulation systems or refrigerate our food. The licensing agency would shut us down the following day. Then they'd relocate our kids to orphanages with openings. The friends they have here are the only family they've ever known."

"I hope that doesn't happen," replied Shayna-punim. "Good luck getting enough uranium."

I crouched lower behind the bush as she left. I smiled despite my embarrassment. I now knew what my Bar Mitzvah project would be—something that would help the orphanage *and* impress Shayna-punim. I would find fuel for the reactor.

* * *

Between practicing for my Bar Mitzvah, convincing my parents to pay for a fancy party, and working on my mitzvah project, the next few weeks passed in a blur.

I cringed at the thought of calling strangers to ask if they'd donate spare uranium. I thought about changing my project. After all, I was a quitter. It's one of the few things I did well. But I'd vowed to do the opposite.

I daydreamed about Shayna-punim at my Bar Mitzvah. She would stare adoringly at me from the front pew as I masterfully conducted the service, my singing pitch-perfect. She would sit next to me at the party, laughing at my clever jokes and lavishing praise on the food. Her purple eyes would glow when I told her that I saved the orphanage from being shut down. Then the music would start, and I'd ask her to dance. The crowd would part for us as we moved with grace and—Mom's call to the dinner table broke me out of my reverie.

✱ ✱ ✱

I didn't ask Meshuggener for help collecting fuel. This was my mitzvah project, and I had to do the work myself.

Most companies said no, adding to my broad experience with rejection. But each call got a bit easier than the previous one. Eventually, I collected 225 kilograms of uranium yellowcake—fifty kilograms from Kramer Clothiers, seventy-five from Benes Dance Studio, and a hundred from Vandelay Industries. It fit in three small lead jars because uranium was so dense.

Best of all, Shayna-punim accepted my Bar Mitzvah invitation.

✱ ✱ ✱

The day before my Bar Mitzvah and party, I scrambled to get everything ready like a hosenpud bird with one of its heads cut off. I called Meshuggener. "Hey, I've been so focused on the party preparations that I almost forgot about the last step of my mitzvah project. Could you deliver the yellowcake concentrate powder for me?"

"Sure, no problem. I'll come by in an hour."

"Thanks. I knew I could count on you. But it's heavy, so bring an antigravity cart."

✱ ✱ ✱

Although the binary star system Alpha Centauri AB climbed in the pale green sky like every other day, this morning it dawned on my Bar Mitzvah. My family ate breakfast, brushed our fangs, got dressed, and took a helidrone to the synagogue.

The rabbi welcomed us warmly and directed us to the front pew.

My parents sat on either side of me, their faces glowing with pride. I wore a white shirt with poofy sleeves and a dark blue suit, tailored to the varying length of my arms. I had no idea how, but weeks ago, Meshuggener found out that Shayna-punim's favorite color was teal. I had to look up that color before placing a special order. My new kippah and prayer shawl featured teal stripes on a white background. *She'll notice that. I hope.*

Thanks to a good tutor and a lot of practice, I felt surprisingly confident. Unsurprisingly, however, that confidence only lasted until the rabbi called me up to the podium to lead the Sabbath service.

I held the prayer book with two tentacles and gripped the lectern tightly with my others. Though I knew the Hebrew words and melodies, my adolescent voice repeatedly cracked throughout my chanting, alternating between tenor and soprano.

My classmates sat together. Noomin wore a fancy new tuxedo and smiled whenever I sang the wrong note.

Noomin! Don't let him get to you. Do the opposite.

Next came the reading of the Torah scroll. I used a tentacle-shaped silver pointer to keep my place as I chanted, finishing the reading without embarrassing myself. *I did it!*

Meshuggener nodded encouragement. Tears of joy slid slowly down my parents' smiling faces.

My throat tightened. *Don't cry.* I shifted my attention to the computer tablet displaying my Bar Mitzvah speech. I shared with the congregation my interpretation of the Torah portion I'd just read and finished by describing my mitzvah project. My tutor had told me to look at the congregation periodically during my speech to connect with them. I risked a glance at Shayna-punim.

She wore a distracting pink dress that highlighted her lovely purple eyes. She lit up when I mentioned the orphanage.

I almost lost my place staring at her face but managed to finish my speech.

The rest of the service transpired without incident. We all shuffled to the adjacent party hall.

"Great job," said Meshuggener.

At Meshuggener's suggestion, the seating plan placed Shayna-punim at the same table as me and my closest friends. But I couldn't join them because guests kept coming over to congratulate me, give me gifts, and offer me traditional Earth wisdom.

"Words should be weighed, not counted," suggested Mr. Spiel.

Old Mrs. Tuches counseled, "If you have to, you can."

I endured an endless stream of congratulatory back slaps, cheek pinches, and mazel tovs. Robotic servers efficiently rolled out food to the buffet table. My mouth watered at the shiny platters heaped with lox, smoked whitefish, pickled herring, smelt, chub, sable, and sturgeon. My stomach rumbled as my friends filled their plates and feasted.

I returned my attention to the line of well-wishers. There stood Shayna-punim. "You did a great job during the service, Schlimazel. And I'm so glad that you're helping the orphanage."

The old me would have stared at the floor and said nothing. So I did the opposite and seized the moment. "Thanks, Shayna-punim. May I have the first dance with you later?" *I did it!*

She gave me a bright smile, but before she could respond, my mom tapped my back.

"Sorry to interrupt, dear. The photographer is ready to take pictures of the four of us." She called Dad and Nan over with a wave of a tentacle.

Sigh. The photographer escorted us back into the synagogue, posing us for formal family portraits. Then we returned to the party room to pose with each group of guests.

As we approached my classmates' table, Noomin shared his opinion that stuffed toys made poor centerpieces.

Noomin!

Before I could defend my choice (and impress Shayna-punim in the process), the photographer swept us along to another table. I felt like a toy boat on a fast-flowing river. In passing, I noted that the buffet table looked like it had been attacked by a pack of hungry vibblegroot wolves.

Old Mrs. Schnorrer, well known for her foraging, snatched up the remaining fish fragments, wrapped them in napkins, and stuffed them in her overcoat pockets. She scooted away when serving robots glided in to replace the now-empty platters with trays of desserts.

My eyes widened at the oval, white plates stacked wondrously high with rugelach, black-and-white cookies, macaroons, hamantashen, and mandelbrot. I considered what excuse I could offer my parents to escape the photographer. *I could say I'm getting a plate of desserts for my friends. That would kill two squillians with one stone. I could finally eat something. And it would give me a chance to tell Shayna-punim I'd be giving her the toys to donate to the orphanage.* Plus, the music would be starting soon. I wanted my dance with Shayna-punim.

The DJ started the first song. Trios shuffled toward the dance floor. *Hey, that's Dr. Nosh! I didn't know he worked as a DJ.* I excused myself.

Meshuggener joined me as I hurried toward the dessert table. "That's quite an impressive pile of pastries. But where's the yellow cake?"

"Huh?"

Meshuggener raised an eyebrow. "You know, the yellow cake powder you had me bring here? I figured it was for a special cake. I delivered it yesterday."

Oh no!

My hearts raced. I grabbed Meshuggener by the arms. "That wasn't yellow cake, it was yellowcake. One word—as in nuclear reactor fuel. It was for the Glick Orphanage!"

"I'm so sorry, Schlimazel."

My empty stomach twisted. I closed my eyes. "It's not your fault, Meshuggener. I was so busy with everything going on, I forgot to tell you where to take it."

Meshuggener lifted three arms. "What's the big deal? Can't we deliver it to the orphanage tomorrow?"

I had to raise my voice to be heard. "No. If I don't get it to them by 5:00 p.m. today, the government's going to shut them down. Those poor kids will get scattered to half a dozen other orphanages. They'll be separated from the only friends they've ever known."

Meshuggener nodded. "But if you leave now—"

"Then I miss my chance to dance with Shayna-punim and tell her about donating the toys," I completed the sentence. "Ugh, I worked hard to plan this party so it would be the perfect chance to impress her."

Is this day supposed to be about me or some strangers? My mind drifted to the Torah portion I'd chanted today, Re'eh. My Bar Mitzvah speech discussed striking a balance between caring for others and caring for oneself.

Meshuggener stood motionless, awaiting my decision.

I paced. *It's not really about one day. It's about becoming responsible from this day forward.*

Meshuggener tapped a tentacle impatiently. "Schlimazel, it's almost four o'clock! What should we do?"

"Take me to the yellowcake," I said, hoping it hadn't already been baked into a dessert or thrown in the trash.

We hurried to the kitchen. "Where'd you leave the cart?" I asked.

"I gave it to someone, but I didn't see what they did with it."

We scrambled through the kitchen, finally locating the cart, tucked away in a corner. I unscrewed the jar tops. "Good. It's all here."

"Now what?" Meshuggener asked.

I leaned in. "I'm supposed to be responsible for my own actions. And today's just as big a day for my parents as it is for me. So I'm not going to ask one of them to leave the party to take me to the orphanage. I'll slip out the back door and call a hypertaxi."

"How will you pay for the ride there and back?"

"I have cash," I replied, tapping my jacket breast pocket. "Uncle Leeyo's Bar Mitzvah gift."

A smile split Meshugenner's face. "Okay, let's go."

I grabbed an arm. "You're a good friend. But I need you here. If anyone notices I'm gone, you give an excuse, like 'I saw him in the kitchen' or 'maybe he's in the bathroom.'"

"Got it. Good luck, Schlimazel."

I put my kippah in my pocket, switched on the cart's antigravity, and rolled it out the kitchen back door and to the street. I left it in hover mode right above the curb. I took my communicator out of my jacket and requested a hypertaxi.

Expected arrival time: seven minutes flashed on my screen. A beep indicated a new message arrived. It was from the photographer, addressed to me and my parents. *That was quick.*

I clicked the link and sorted through over one hundred Bar Mitzvah images, looking for any with Shayna-punim in them.

I was so engrossed by a picture of her smiling and giving the tentacles-up sign that I didn't notice the vehicle until it was nearly on top of me.

The enormous green robotic street cleaner, designed to suck up debris from curbside, gobbled up the cart with the yellowcake.

No!

The street cleaner rolled away. Paralyzed, I recalled the Earth expression *I need this like a hole in the head.* The old me would have quit right there. But I was no longer the old me. *Go!*

I chased the slow-moving vehicle, weaving through wide-eyed pedestrians, my arms flailing. "Pardon me. Excuse me. So sorry."

I closed the gap and made a leap of faith. Suckers at the tip of one arm stuck to the rear bumper. Holding on for dear life, I hauled myself onto the back of the vehicle. I stood on the bumper and gasped for breath. *Now what?*

You've got a vehicle. Use it.

I spread six tentacles wide for better traction and worked my way forward along the curb-facing side of the vehicle. *Look out!*

I flattened against the vehicle to avoid getting smashed by a mailbox on the street corner. *Too close!* But those orphans needed my help.

Although the street cleaner needed no driver, it had a cockpit where maintenance staff could run computer diagnostics and software updates. I hauled myself into the cramped space and scanned the cockpit interface. *These controls are just like the vehicle simulation game I play.* My eyes landed on a toggle switch labeled MANUAL CONTROL. *That's it!* I threw the switch and grabbed the steering yoke with four arms. Using the map on my communicator, I herded the mechanical beast toward the orphanage. But even at the cleaner's maximum speed, passenger vehicles still swept past. *Too slow.*

I kept one eye on the road and the other on the time. *Come on. Come on.* Finally, the orphanage came into view. I parked in front and searched the interface. *There!* I pressed the OPEN GARBAGE HATCH button.

I scrambled to the rear of the street cleaner. The good news was that the trash had not yet been compacted. The bad news was that the garbage container was half-full of garbage. *Hurry. You're almost out of time!*

Yanking off my suit jacket, I climbed into the filthy compartment.

I spotted the cart and dragged it out of the vehicle, setting it directly under the open hatch. *Now, how am I going to find three small jars? They're small…but they're also heavy. They probably settled to the bottom. Dig!* My tentacles burrowed through the trash.

There! Using all my strength, I rolled the jars one at a time out of the hatch and onto the antigravity cart. *Go!*

I raced to the orphanage's front door.

"Hello," the receptionist said before recoiling from my smudged face.

"Hi. I'm here to donate two hundred and twenty-five kilograms of yellowcake," I replied. Then I gave her a triumphant smile.

Suddenly, my appearance no longer mattered. "Oh, how wonderful." Her eyes glistened. "You're just in time. We'll rush these over to be processed into fuel rods right away. Thank you. Thank you!"

I smiled. My communicator indicated 4:47 p.m. "Glad to help. Please excuse me. There's a mess on the curb I need to clean up."

✱ ✱ ✱

By the time I rushed back to my party and put on my jacket and kippah, the DJ had finished packing up his equipment. Nothing remained of the desserts. Half the guests had left. *Sigh.*

Meshugenner raced over. "Well?"

"I made it!" I replied, raising a tentacle in victory.

Meshuggener pulled me in for a hug, oblivious to my stained

shirt. "I want to hear the whole story. But first, someone else wants to talk with you."

Great. I'm going to have to explain my dirty clothes to Mom, Dad, and Nan.

The petite Shayna-punim emerged from behind Meshuggener, eyeing me up and down.

"Hi, Schlimazel. I like your teal kippah. And I saved you some treats." She offered me a small plate with chocolate-dipped macaroons.

I was speechless. Both from the embarrassing state of my suit and her radiant smile.

"Meshuggener told me you're giving me the centerpiece toys to donate to the orphanage. And also that you skipped your own party to help the orphans." Her purple eyes glowed. "But I was disappointed."

"Disappointed?" My stomach knotted.

"Yes. I wanted to dance with you, but we never had the chance. So will you come to my Bat Mitzvah?"

My hearts raced. "Yes, I'd love to."

Author's Note

Schlimazel's lack of confidence was inspired by the George Costanza character from the TV series *Seinfeld.* For the amusement of readers, there are a number of *Seinfeld* parodies in this story. Did you spot them? Here's an easy one: Noomin is a nod to Seinfeld's nemesis, Newman.

The fictional planet Latke orbits the real star, Proxima Centauri, which is 4.24 light years from Earth. Einstein's theory of special relativity tells us that a spaceship able to travel at 99 percent of the speed of light will experience a time dilation (Lorentz) factor of 7.1. In other words, 7.1 years pass on Latke for every year that an astronaut travels at that speed. So, about sixty-three years passed on Latke while their astronauts aged eight and a half years (4.24 years each way). Although it sounds like science fiction, time dilation has been repeatedly proven by experiments.

Meshuggener's reactor fuel confusion is understandable, since yellow cake *is* a tasty treat. But yellowcake (one word) refers to uranium concentrate powder that can be used to prepare fuel for nuclear reactors. Yellowcake is 70 to 90 percent triuranium octoxide (U_3O_8). Although not especially radioactive, yellowcake is roughly forty-seven times denser than water and you'd need an oven that could heat to 2880 °C just to melt it. These factors suggest it would make a terrible dessert.

Where Is Uncle Louie?

Alan Katz

My Bar Mitzvah reception wasn't very festive, but in my parents' judgment, it was going swimmingly. The food at the Hillside House was fine (well, as fine as $4.95 a person for a complete meal could buy).

Jack Watson was cranking out the hits of the early seventies on his accordion (my parents had no interest in booking a band, and although the letters D and J had been invented, they weren't yet used together in relation to party entertainment).

Cousin Marty was taking black-and-white Polaroid instant photos (each one was blurrier than the one before, but at least you could see the disappointing blurriness sixty seconds after the picture was taken).

Most of the adult tables were subdued, filled with polite, quiet conversation. My table of friends, however, was noisy. Extremely noisy. At one point, my father's sister, Irene, asked them to "pipe down." Although some of them didn't seem to know what she meant by that, they respectfully lowered their voices.

Then they quietly started flinging stewed tomatoes at each other. I'll never forget the look on Michael Braverman's face when a tomato smashed onto his lapel and slid straight down his sports jacket—the jacket that still had the price tags on the sleeve because his mother was planning to return it the next day. I never found out how that worked out for him, but the situation—like the tomatoey jacket—wasn't pretty.

By the way, there wasn't any dancing at my Bar Mitzvah. Reception Room A had a slab of wood in the floor, but it was no bigger than a diving board. What's more, no one in the history of mankind has been dance-deprived enough to "get down" to the sounds of an accordion. Go ahead—download some accordion music and try to do a funky dance. It's simply not possible.

Why did we have a party in a room without any space to dance? Well, two years before, when my parents booked the facility for my party, the manager of the Hillside House tried to steer us to Reception Room B or Reception Room C. He said that Room A was mostly used for business meetings that didn't require a dance floor.

But when he told us that you had to go up a few stairs to get to Rooms B and C, my mother said, "No. We have senior citizens coming to the party, and we don't want elderly people to have to climb steps." The manager asked, "How many senior citizens could you possibly have at a thirteen-year-old's Bar Mitzvah reception?" When my mother told him, "Five or so," he responded, "Well, the party is two years away. Maybe they'll be dead by then."

I swear that's true. My mother's jaw dropped. So did my father's. They were aghast and thought about storming out to find another facility. But the Hillside House was walking distance to Temple Israel (where my service was held), so we stayed. Convenience won out. And it didn't hurt that the manager saw that they were upset and gave them a discount on Room A.

So there wasn't any dancing. My Bar Mitzvah party also didn't include any contests, prizes, or giveaways. At my kids' Bar and Bat Mitzvahs, we gave away more merchandise than they do during a whole season of *The Price Is Right*. These days, kids have competitions to see who gives better stuff; my daughter once came home from a Bat Mitzvah with a live hermit crab (not kosher!) with her name painted on its shell.

We gave nothing, absolutely nothing to my friends—other than Michael Braverman, who left with the two-foot-long tomato smear on his jacket.

But it was still a fine party. The seventy-five people in attendance were having a good enough time.

Until, that is, there were seventy-four of us.

It wasn't as if anyone literally counted. But not long after the salad had been served (that's where the stewed tomatoes came from), Cousin Barbara noticed that her father was…

Missing.

Barbara said she'd been with him throughout the hors d'oeuvre hour (which actually lasted only forty-five minutes. Plus, they ran out of cocktail franks within minutes. And the mustard was frozen. My mother was keeping a list of such grievances against the Hillside House; boy, was she going to complain about all of that on Monday!).

But Barbara hadn't seen her father since the hors d'oeuvres had been served. She cried out for him: "Has anyone seen Louie?" And her call spread like wildfire. From table to table and from generation to generation, people said things like "Louie?" and "Where's Louie?" The kids at my friends table all yelled, "Who's Louie?"

Jack Watson, perhaps playing at and attending his first Bar Mitzvah ever, must have thought people were asking him to play the 1963 rock 'n' roll hit "Louie Louie." He looked in his fake book—a book that party musicians consult to fake their way through songs by using simple chords—and played it as best he could. Based on that performance, I'm sure my parents wanted to pay him with fake money.

But back to Uncle Louie.

He was nowhere to be found. This eighty-five-year-old gentleman had seemingly disappeared into thin (accordion music–filled) air.

Maybe it was because I'd said the words "Today I am a man" just hours earlier. But I remember so clearly that I was the one to suggest that Louie wasn't missing; he was likely just visiting the men's room.

Barbara brightened at the thought.

"The men's room. Sure! That's where he is! He's got to be there!

He spends a lot of time in the men's room! At eighty-five, it sometimes takes him longer to do his business."

I wished she hadn't told me that part. I also wondered what kind of business he did in the men's room, but I didn't tell her that.

Barbara kissed me and said, "Alan, be a dear and go fetch my father from the men's room!"

Sending me out of my own party seemed weird. Still, I did as asked. Barbara was about thirty years older than I was, but I always liked her. And I didn't want her to be worried. So I made my way to the men's room, where I'd also be sure to wash off the lipstick she'd just plastered onto my cheek.

Yes, on my big day, I stepped into the restroom and blurted out, "Louie? Uncle Louie?"

No one answered.

I ran past the stalls, ducking down to see if anyone's feet were visible. No feet. No people. No Louie.

Then I gently kicked in the stall doors—James Bond style—to see if maybe Louie was sitting inside one of the stalls, "doing his business" with his feet high in the air.

There was no business.

And no Louie.

I washed my face. Slowly. Because I was in no hurry to get back to Barbara and tell her that her missing father was still missing.

In a fit of inspiration, I left the restroom, left the Hillside House, and went outside. Maybe Uncle Louie had gone out for a breath of fresh air (though that wasn't likely, since it was raining very hard and the air was pretty dense with fog).

At any rate, it was a good try. And it delayed my having to go back to my party Louie-less. Extremely Louie-less. I didn't have any Louie at all.

As I walked back into the building, I had a lot on my mind. I knew I'd soon have to recite the candle-lighting poems to honor family members. I'd written them the night before, and I was afraid they were pretty weak.

What else was I thinking about? Well, believe it or not, I was worried about all of the thank-you cards I'd have to write. I knew that people were likely going to be generous gift-wise, and I knew that my mother was going to make me write thank-yous—probably starting that very night.

But back to Uncle Louie.

I stood in the lobby of the Hillside House and stared at the door to Reception Room A. Behind that door was a party *for me*. But I wasn't partying. I was searching for a man I hardly knew. I'd probably spent a total of five hours with Uncle Louie in my entire life.

I remembered being with him at his daughter's house; it might have been for his eightieth birthday party. I thought about the trick he did: he showed me a glass of apple juice, and said, "Want to see me drink this juice without touching the glass at all?"

I said, "That's not possible."

He said, "It is possible, and you're about to see me do it."

"I bet you can't."

"How much do you want to bet? A hundred dollars?"

I told him, "I don't have a hundred dollars."

This went on for a long time. We finally settled on betting a quarter. We wagered twenty-five cents than he couldn't drink his apple juice without touching the glass.

We each put a quarter on the table.

"You ready?" he asked.

"I'm ready," I said.

"Okay, here goes."

Then…he took out a straw and slurped the juice through it.

When he'd finished, he burped. Then he hiccupped. Then he said, "Finished. And my fingers never touched the glass."

He winked. He patted me on the head. Then he took my quarter and popped it into his pocket.

"You're really going to take my quarter?" I asked him.

"Yes, you need to learn that you shouldn't bet!" he told me. "What are you, five years old? Six?"

"I'm eight," I informed him. "I used to be eight and a quarter, but now I'm just eight."

"*How is it possible* you're not eight and a quarter anymore?" he wanted to know.

"You took my quarter," I said.

Then I winked.

That really happened. And I want to tell you that he smiled so widely that he gave me back my quarter—plus an extra dollar.

I want to tell you that.

But that's not what he did.

Nope. He frowned, kept the money, and said, "Go on, get outta here before I call a policeman."

I remember those words like it was yesterday. And that was the man I was in charge of finding at my Bar Mitzvah reception.

I desperately didn't want to go back into Reception Room A and face Barbara. I just didn't have the words to tell her that her father was still missing. But there was nowhere else to go, except...

Reception Room B or Reception Room C. Each had a party just like mine going on. Well, not *exactly* just like mine. Because after I climbed the (three measly) steps up to Room B and stood outside the entrance, I heard a band. Or maybe it was an orchestra. They were playing "Hava Nagila," and it sounded awesome. Then I went down the hallway (and up one more step) to Room C. I didn't even have to go inside to know that they were having the party of the year.

As I said, I didn't *have* to go inside. And yet, that's just what I did. I simply had to see what a *lively* Bar Mitzvah reception looked like. A sign next to the door said "Stanley Mandel's Big Bar Mitzvah Party." The word "expensive" wasn't written there, but it was sure implied. (In contrast, the sign on the door to Room A said "Katz.")

I just had to go inside. I told myself that I had to look as if I belonged there; if anyone asked, I'd say I was Stanley's long-lost cousin. I wasn't going to eat anything. I wasn't going to bother anyone. I just wanted to look around, take it all in, then go back and face the "Uncle Louie is still missing" situation.

I stepped inside of Reception Room C. And let me tell you, putting it in terms of fun, if my party room was a simple backyard carnival, Stanley's was…Disneyland meets Six Flags meets twelve other theme parks.

I looked around and saw an eight-piece band and three spirited, talented singers. A buffet table filled with hors d'oeuvres as far as the eye could see (including buckets of mustard—not frozen), and a bust of Stanley's head made out of chopped liver (quite a good likeness).

It was a party filled with energy. I saw people dancing. I saw people excitedly chatting. I saw everyone having an amazing time. And then, I saw…

Uncle Louie!

My Uncle Louie!

At Stanley's party!

I didn't want to make a scene, but I rushed up to him, took him by the arm, and said, "Uncle Louie!"

He smiled and said, "I know you!"

I said, "Of course, you do. I'm Alan. And everyone's looking for you."

"Well," he responded. "I'm right here. And I'm having a wonderful time."

"That's great, Uncle Louie," I told him. "But we have to go!"

"Go?!" he boomed. "But I'm having a swell time! Music! Dancing! Chopped liver!"

I explained that it was indeed a fine party, but that it wasn't *my* party. It wasn't the party to which he'd been invited.

"No one's kicking me out!" he insisted. "Go on, get outta here before I call a policeman."

But I held my ground and escorted him out of Reception Room C (I admit it, I grabbed a mini knish), then slowly helped him down the stairs and walked him to the door of my party.

Along the way, he told me that he'd gone to the bathroom. And after he'd done his business, he left the bathroom and must have made a wrong turn and ended up at Reception Room C. He didn't remember that my party was on the same level as the bathroom ("some nice boys walked me up the steps"). He didn't notice the Stanley Mandel sign. And he didn't know—or didn't care—that he'd been partying surrounded by strangers.

He asked one more time: "Couldn't we go back to that *fancy* party?" But I said no and walked him into the room marked "Katz."

The room was dark and silent. Jack Watson was taking a break; he was sitting on his accordion case, demolishing a plateful of cocktail franks (*so that's where they'd gone!*). There was a palpable scent of worry in the air. And then, Barbara turned to face the light shining in from the door I'd opened…saw her father…and *shrieked*, "Louie! Alan found Louie!"

Everyone screamed "Louie!" I explained where I'd located him.

Barbara kissed me for being so smart (ugh, more lipstick!).

And suddenly, the party was on!

It still wasn't all that great a Bar Mitzvah reception. The food didn't change. There still wasn't any dancing. And Jack was forced to admit that he didn't know how to play "Hava Nagila."

But it was suddenly an "Alan found Louie!" celebration. And that made it a party to remember.

My candle-lighting ceremony went perfectly. My rhymes were well received, and when it was time to call Uncle Louie to light a candle, we both said something memorable:

I skipped the (probably cheesy) rhyme I'd written to ask him to join me and spontaneously made up a poem. With the whole room silent and waiting to hear what I'd say, I announced…

I'd like to call up Uncle Louie
For a family honor he truly deserves.
I'm so glad he's back at the party with us
After hitting Room C for better hors d'oeuvres.

I got thunderous applause. I was even asked to repeat it as Louie made his way to the candles.

And as he stood beside me, he said, "At least you're having me light a candle. They didn't ask me to do that at that other party!"

Louie got a standing ovation.

I wanted to tell him, *Go on, get outta here before I call a policeman.*

But I didn't.

I hugged him. He hugged me. And the party continued joyously.

And as I reflect on the day, I'm filled with gratitude. Gratitude for my parents, who threw the very best party they could. We weren't a flashy, Room C–type family. We had basic tastes, and though I would've loved to see my head sculpted into chopped liver, Room A was just right for us.

I'm also grateful to Cousin Marty, who had a crappy, crappy camera but a strong sense of family. His work as a Bar Mitzvah photographer meant the world to me, and he still means the world to me. I cherish the blurry, faded, crappy, crappy photos he took that day.

I'm grateful to Harold Borden, who threw the stewed tomato at Michael Braverman's sport jacket. The mental image still makes me howl with laughter.

I'm grateful that on the very day I started my journey into being a responsible adult, I was given an opportunity to come through for the family in a big way.

And I'm grateful to everyone who spent the afternoon of April 18, 1970, in Room A at the Hillside House. That building is no longer a catering hall; it's a carpet store. But that's okay. I still have the memories.

The Contest

Nancy Krulik

"Shabbat Shalom. Welcome to my Bar Mitzvah. Today I promise to make it all the way through the service without getting asked to leave the sanctuary."

From the corner of my eye, I can see my mother cringing as I say the opening line of my d'var Torah. That's not how she wanted me to start my discussion of my Torah portion. But the rabbi said I should be myself in my speech. And that is the kid who, for months now, has been thrown out of the main sanctuary by the ushers for misbehaving during services on purpose.

Yeah, you read right. *On purpose.*

It all started at the beginning of seventh grade when my classmates and I began attending one another's B'nai Mitzvah. (I used to say Bar and Bat Mitzvahs, but my Hebrew teacher, Morah Chava, goes bananas when anyone says that.) I go to a Jewish day school, so every single person in my class was going to have a B'nai Mitzvah. And the rule is you have to invite everyone in the grade to your service and celebration. That's a lot of services. Which means a lot of sitting. And listening. Neither of which I'm particularly good at. My grandfather says I have shpilkes, which basically means I can never keep still.

It's not like I didn't start out trying to behave for a whole service. I mean, when you put on a jacket and a tie, you kind of feel more adult than usual to begin with, right? And then when you add the kippah as you walk into the sanctuary, you know you're *supposed* to be praying. The kippah is a sign of respect, after all.

I definitely know the prayers for Shabbat. These services have always been a part of my life: from the nursery school Tot Shabbats to Friday morning school services, to being in the junior, junior choir and then the junior choir, both of which perform one Friday night a month at the synagogue.

But being in a choir is different. We kids are all lined up right there on the stairs that lead to the bimah, right in front of the ark where the Torahs are kept. When you're on the bimah, that close to the Torah, with everyone watching, you're more likely to behave yourself, right? Not to mention the fact that every time one of the choirs performed, my parents were right there, sitting in a row near the front, listening to us sing—with their eyes aimed straight at me.

That's not the way it is at the Saturday morning services. For one thing, there are no kids' choirs performing on Shabbat morning. And for another, unless our parents are specifically invited, most of them don't attend every single B'nai Mitzvah. They drop us off, and we go into the main sanctuary by ourselves. That means it's just us kids, sitting in the back rows, hanging out—with no one but the volunteer ushers to keep an eye on us.

I would never want the ushers' jobs. It's got to be tough keeping an eye on everyone and making sure the service goes on uninterrupted. Especially since you've usually got three full rows of twelve- and thirteen-year-olds sitting close together. Let's face it, my classmates and I aren't exactly what you'd call model congregants.

Now, in our defense, there are a lot of rules to follow in the main sanctuary of my temple. For starters, you can't text or look at your phone—even if you've kept it on silent. If the ushers catch a kid staring at his phone they threaten to take it away—and I've seen them do it. I think they give the phones back at the end of the service—I mean they'd have to, right? But there's no guarantee. So that's one rule I try to follow.

Then there's the no-talking rule. Not even whispering. Which isn't easy. Especially when I'm sitting next to my best friend, Michael. Michael can *really* talk. About anything. To anyone. I'll bet he even talks in his sleep.

Which is why from the beginning of the "Bar Mitzvah season" (as my father calls the weekly celebrations marked on our family calendar), it was Michael who was almost always the first of my group of friends to be asked by one of the ushers to leave the sanctuary. That was usually soon followed by an usher requesting that my friends Teddy, Jack, Andrew, and I leave as well. Which we did. Without argument.

But it was Michael who turned getting thrown out of the sanctuary into an actual contest. I remember the morning he started the whole thing. It was right after my friends and I had been asked to leave the sanctuary around the middle of Evan Rubenstein's Bar Mitzvah service. Michael was standing alone outside by the slide in the little kids' playground, when Teddy, Jack, Andrew, and I came walking out.

"What took you so long?" he asked. "I was thrown out hours ago."

"It's only been five minutes," Andrew told him.

"Actually seven," I corrected him. I smiled as I pointed to my watch. I can be very exacting like that—especially when I felt like being annoying. Which I did.

Michael and Andrew both rolled their eyes at me.

Mission accomplished.

"Yeah, well, I was the first one thrown out today," Michael bragged. I think he even puffed his chest out a little bit. "I'm *always* the first one thrown out."

Thinking back, I'm not sure why Michael was so proud of that fact. But at the time it definitely seemed like some sort of accomplishment.

My friends and I are very competitive, so now we all wanted to beat Michael to it next time. The contest had begun. Michael was practically daring us to try and beat him to be the first one thrown out of services. So what else could I do? What else would *any* self-respecting, almost thirteen-year-old guy do?

The next week, it was Rachel S.'s Bat Mitzvah (not to be confused with Rachel C., who had had her Bat Mitzvah two weeks before), and this time I was determined to be the first one to be thrown out.

Unfortunately, so were all my friends.

As usual, it was Michael who was the first one to start talking. "Do you think the Yankees have a shot this year?" he asked Teddy.

I couldn't believe it. Michael had guts. The service had literally just begun. We were only halfway through the Ma Tovu prayer, and he was already at it. Talk about wanting to win. My friends and I are usually able to get a little closer to the Torah service part of the morning before we start getting antsy in our seats.

Michael sure knew what he was doing bringing up the Yankees. Teddy's a dedicated Mets fan, and everyone knows it. The Mets and the Yankees are New York's home team rivals. There was no way Teddy was going to let Michael's question pass without a slam on the Yanks.

"If the Yankees do get into the World Series, it'll be because they bought their way in," Teddy answered. He pretty much says the same thing every time Michael or I bring up the Yankees. "The salaries they pay their top players are ridiculous."

"You're just jealous," Michael said a little more loudly. "The Yankees always have a better shot at winning than the Mets. Everybody knows..."

That's when the usher started heading toward us. Michael wasn't even *trying* to whisper anymore. He was making a proclamation. And the people around us had all turned around to stare. The usher looked plenty mad.

Mad enough to throw Michael out before the rest of us.

There was no way I was letting that happen. I had to do something. Something that would get me kicked out. But not something so bad that I would be kicked out forever. (Not that I was sure you *could* get kicked out of a synagogue forever, but I wasn't taking the chance.)

So as the usher got closer, I took a deep breath. I mean I really sucked a whole bunch of air into my belly. And then...

BURP!

I let out a belch. It was a decent-sized gas explosion. Not my biggest (I mean, I was in a *synagogue,* after all). But certainly it was big enough to start my friends laughing—just as I was sure it would. I know we're all in seventh grade, and we're supposed to be more mature than we were when we were in elementary school, but a good burp never ceases to crack us up. I've seen a burp make my dad laugh so hard his face turns beet red. There are some things you just don't outgrow.

The people sitting in the row in front of us turned around and gave us dirty looks. I smiled at them and tried to choke back my laughter. "Excuse me," I apologized as the usher got closer. "I had a really big breakfast. It must have upset my stomach."

That started my friends laughing all over again.

The usher shook her head. "You boys have no respect," she whispered. "Not for the synagogue. Or the congregation. Or your classmate up there on the bimah. You should be ashamed of yourselves."

And for a minute, I was. Maybe we *were* taking this whole thing a little too far. I was working on learning my Torah and haftarah portions, and I knew what kind of an effort that was. I'd listened to the recording of the cantor's voice so many times I swear I'd been chanting my portion in my sleep. I'd also just started to think about my d'var Torah, which wasn't easy either. Writing that speech was proving to be harder than any report I'd ever had to write for school. I hadn't even come up with my opening line yet. Rachel had surely worked as hard on her Bat Mitzvah preparation. Maybe harder. I'd heard that she had to practice learning her portion with a rabbi while she was away at summer camp. Now *that's* dedication.

My friends and I probably should have tried to stay and at least hear Rachel chant her portion. But as I looked up at the usher, I could tell that wasn't how this was going to play out. She'd had it with me being disruptive. So out I went. My friends followed only a few minutes later. They were still laughing as they met me on the playground.

I actually felt a little bad about the whole thing, until Teddy told me, "That burp was excellent."

"Perfect timing, bro," Andrew agreed.

"Dude, I really thought I was going to lose it when I saw that usher's face," Michael added. "That belch was a work of art."

"Yeah," Jack replied. "You're like the Michelangelo of gas."

That was high praise. I felt a little like the way a movie star must feel when he gets a really good review.

"I definitely won this week," I boasted. But for some reason I didn't feel as victorious as I thought I would. In fact, I was a little embarrassed. Just not so embarrassed that I was going to give up on the contest.

None of us were.

And so the game went on. Week after week. Some Shabbat mornings I was the first one out. Other times it was one of my friends. We never knew for sure who would be the contest winner on any given week. We just knew that by the middle of the service, we'd all be out on the playground, having a whole lot more fun than we would have sitting in the sanctuary—unless of course it rained, in which case we just hung out in the men's room. Which wasn't nearly as fun.

The one Shabbat I took a break from the contest was for Michael's Bar Mitzvah. I made it almost the whole way through that one. After all, he's my best friend. Also my parents were invited to his Bar Mitzvah, and I don't think they'd have appreciated watching their son be thrown out of services in real time. So I waited until after Michael had given his d'var Torah and chanted his portion before I excused myself to go to the bathroom. I didn't come back until the service was almost over.

My parents didn't say anything to me directly about that. But my dad did mention what a shame it was that I'd missed the rabbi's sermon. I'm pretty sure that was his way of letting me know he'd noticed I'd disappeared on them.

Okay, so by now I'm figuring you're thinking my friends and I had been behaving like a bunch of spoiled brats. And you'd be right. But you could also say we were just a bunch of kids acting like kids. Maybe not kids who were "on the precipice of adulthood" as my Jewish Studies teacher, Moreh Goldman, likes to say, but kids just the same.

I can't tell you how many times I've heard Moreh Goldman talk about the whole "significance of the B'nai Mitzvah" thing. But I can tell you, it didn't seem particularly real to me. I'm sure there was once a time when being thirteen made you an adult in Jewish society, but that time isn't now. The teachers in school didn't suddenly start treating my friends who had already read from the Torah like adults and neither did their parents. They weren't given any additional responsibilities or privileges. Most of them still had a designated bedtime, which isn't exactly adult-like, is it?

I thought about asking my friends who'd already been called to the Torah as a Bar Mitzvah if they felt any different, but I didn't. It's just not the kind of thing one guy asks another. Besides, they weren't *acting* any more spiritual or mature. The first Shabbat after his Bar Mitzvah, Michael went right back to taking part in our contest—with a vengeance. He'd managed to get himself thrown out of Sam Sapperstein's Bar Mitzvah before the service even started. And he was really proud of it. Since I knew that our contest could be considered kind of childish, it was clear to me that Michael hadn't suddenly, miraculously become a man just because he'd put on his grandfather's tallit and said a few prayers in front of the congregation.

The Monday morning after Sam's Bar Mitzvah, my classmate Leah walked over to Michael and me right before homeroom. She had an angry look on her face.

"You guys better not cause trouble at my Bat Mitzvah next weekend," she told us. "I have a special guest coming to talk to the congregation. You'll look like real jerks if you pull your usual stuff at my service. So don't."

"Let me guess, your mom's gonna give a speech," Michael said while rolling his eyes.

I laughed. Her mom probably wasn't the guest Leah was talking about. There wouldn't be anything special about that. Leah's mom was on the synagogue board. She'd spoken at services before.

"Nope, it's not my mom," Leah said. "And that's all I'm saying. I'm not telling you anything else."

As Leah walked away, Michael and I looked at each other with surprise.

"Do you think Leah's family knows someone famous?" I asked him. "Like maybe an actor or a ball player?"

"I doubt it," Michael replied. "Leah would have bragged about something like that *way* before this."

That was true. Bragging was really Leah's thing.

So now I was curious. What special guest could Leah have invited to her Bat Mitzvah? It had to be someone really important. Once in a while someone from the synagogue board, like Leah's mom, made an announcement at the end of services. (Not that my friends and I were ever still in services by the time *that* happened, but Leah boasted about it a lot.) Still, as far as I knew, we hadn't had a guest speaker before.

When Saturday morning came, I wasn't particularly anxious to be thrown out—at least not until I figured out who the celebrity was Leah had been boasting about. But as I scanned the faces of the people entering the sanctuary, not one looked familiar. I didn't see a tall basketball player or a familiar face from TV or the movies.

"I think Leah was making it all up," Michael told me. "She just wanted attention."

"She *always* wants attention," Jack replied.

I wasn't so sure. Leah had been pretty convincing when she'd spoken to Michael and me. So I was determined to stick around to find out what was going on.

Apparently I was the only one of my friends who felt that way, because when the time came for the Torah service, I was the only one of us still left in the sanctuary. I was waiting to see who was going to speak.

I stood up with the rest of the congregation as the rabbi and the cantor went to the ark and opened the curtains. Then they each took out a Torah and began to walk around the synagogue. People rushed to the aisles with prayer books in hand to kiss the Torah. As the rabbi walked close to where I was standing, he looked at me curiously—almost with surprise. Not that I blamed him. With all my friends already gone and my parents nowhere in sight, he was probably shocked to see me.

Frankly, I was beginning to feel like maybe I shouldn't have bothered sticking around. The reading of the Torah comes pretty far into the service, and I still hadn't had a single celebrity sighting. So by the time the cantor placed the Torah down and opened it to the correct portion, I was pretty much ready to walk out.

But the truth is, even *I* understood that once the Torah was open and about to be read, it was too disrespectful to walk out. So I waited and listened for the cantor to chant and call Leah to the Torah as a Bat Mitzvah.

Except the cantor *didn't* call Leah to the Torah. Leah's Hebrew name is Leah, just like her English name. That's not the name our cantor chanted. Instead, she called the name Rivkah. I know the Hebrew name of every single person in our grade. I've been hearing them since I was in kindergarten. And there's no Rivkah.

Leah's dad got up and walked across the aisle to where an older woman was struggling to stand. Older wasn't even the right word. This woman was just old. Really, *really* old. She had skin so wrinkled and thin it looked like the tissue paper you find in shoeboxes. Her hair was bright orange, but I knew that couldn't be her real color. I'd never seen anyone with hair like that—especially not someone that old.

I watched as the woman held tight to Leah's father's arm, and together they walked up to the bimah. The woman took small, slow steps, and it was actually painful to watch her go up the stairs. When she finally reached the lectern, the old woman held on for support. "Boker Tov," she said. "Good Shabbos."

Shabbos? I figured she meant Shabbat. But with her accent, she sounded like a character in the movie *Fiddler on the Roof* I'd watched at my grandfather's house once.

"I am Leah's great-grandmother Rivkah, and I am so glad to be here this morning," the old woman continued. "Of course, at my age, I'm glad to be anywhere this morning."

The grown-ups in the congregation all started laughing. It was their kind of joke. I didn't find it particularly funny. But I *was* fascinated by Leah's great-grandmother. I didn't know anyone else who had a great-grandmother who was still alive. Even if this special guest wasn't a ball player or a musician, it was still really cool to hear her talk.

"I am so grateful that Leah has agreed to share her special day with me because I have waited my entire life to be called to the Torah as a Bat Mitzvah," Leah's great grandmother told the congregation. "You see, when I was thirteen and living in the Soviet Union, girls couldn't have a Bat Mitzvah. Boys weren't really allowed to have a Bar Mitzvah either, but sometimes they had them in secret, hiding in someone's tiny apartment with the doors locked and the curtains drawn. It was quite a brave thing to do, because if they were caught, everyone present at the service could have been arrested."

A secret Bar Mitzvah.

Because a Bar Mitzvah was against the law.

Wow. That was just crazy.

I'd heard of the Soviet Union. We'd learned about it in history class. It was a huge country made up of fifteen states, including Russia, that had previously been their own countries. The Soviet government was communist, which meant everything—the farms, the factories, and even people's homes—was owned by the government.

I remembered reading in my history book that the Soviet government was *very* controlling. A person could go to jail just for criticizing the leaders or the communist way of life. They told authors what they could write and artists what they could paint. The government was also notoriously against religion, and at one point, there was a law that no one under sixteen could participate in any religious ceremony.

It sounded like a horrible place to live.

When we'd been learning about the Soviet Union in history class, it had seemed exactly that—history. Just like the Revolutionary War or the assassination of President Lincoln. After all, the country didn't even exist anymore. In 1991, the Soviet Union had broken apart, and the countries went back to self-rule. So I never dreamed I would actually meet anyone who had lived there. To me, information about the Soviet Union was just something else I had to memorize for a test. It was a place and way of life that had existed long ago and far away. Hearing how it felt from someone who had been there and lived through it was a whole other story.

"It wasn't easy being Jewish in the Soviet Union," Leah's great-grandmother continued. "We weren't liked. Poor treatment of Jews was something that came from the top down. The government didn't consider anti-Semitism a problem to be corrected or outlawed; it was actually *encouraged* by the people in power. Strangely, even though Jews weren't wanted, we weren't allowed to leave either. My family requested a visa to emigrate five times. We were always refused."

That was weird. It seemed to me that if you didn't like people, you wouldn't want them around. Keeping Jews stuck in the Soviet Union just seemed like some sort of way to torture them. Which is probably what it was.

"The excuses the government used to refuse visas for my family were ridiculous," Leah's great-grandmother continued. "They said we might have Soviet secrets, which we most definitely did not. And to make matters worse, once we applied for our visas, my father, who was an engineer, was fired from his job and forced to become a street sweeper. We were hungry, humiliated, and hated. Yet the government would not let us leave. And of course, we still could not pray out in the open as we are all doing today. Back then, we would have given anything to pray in a place such as this."

I squirmed in my seat. I thought about some almost-thirteen-year-old kid in the Soviet Union who had been denied any chance to pray. And here my friends and I had made a game of getting kicked out of the sanctuary.

"When I came to the United States, I heard that some boys in free countries had been having 'twin' B'nai Mitzvah services in our honor," Leah's great-grandmother continued. "They symbolically shared their services with someone in the Soviet Union who could not be called to the Torah. I wish back then we had known this was happening. It would have meant so much to all of us. But of course, the Soviet government told us nothing."

Suddenly, our contest seemed kind of stupid. And immature. Like a game little kids would have played. And my friends and I weren't little anymore. Sure, even though one by one we were being called to the Torah as a Bar Mitzvah, none of us had miraculously become a grown-up. But we were getting there, which meant we should start taking on a little bit of responsibility. We owed it to Leah's great-grandmother Rivkah and the kids she grew up with.

I'd like to be able to tell you that from that day on, I never got asked to leave the sanctuary for misbehaving again. But I'd be lying. Even though I stopped consciously taking part in the contest, I definitely still got in trouble, and once in a while found myself right back out there on the playground during services. What can I say? Self-control isn't exactly my middle name. But I'm working on it. Shpilkes isn't something that's easy to get rid of. I don't know if I'll ever be able to completely sit still or keep from talking to my friends—in services or anywhere else.

One good thing came out of the contest, though. I finally came up with the opening line of my d'var Torah. And even though my mother might be cringing right now as I say it out loud in front of the congregation, the rabbi had actually found it pretty funny when he'd read my speech in his office. He told me he'd had shpilkes during services when he was a kid too. Although I find that hard to believe. Especially since he always seems to be able to make it all the way through services.

And today I will too.

Without Being Asked

Stacie Ramey

The day I found out Wolf Horowitz was moving back to my neighborhood, a month before my Bat Mitzvah, my nightmare began. Wolfie, as both his friends and frenemies called him, had moved away two years ago. The last time I saw him, he was this weird, skinny kid who wore mismatched clothes and tube socks. For an entire school year, he wore only two T-shirts, in what he said at the time was an experiment to see what people said about him, only I thought it was pure laziness and I told him that the day before he moved. The problem was that instead of being insulted, he put his hand over his heart and beamed a sunshiny smile at me. "Aw, Stef, that's so sweet. You *do* think about me."

Darcy, one of my besties, was the one who broke the news about his return. We were packing away our group work, just minutes before the bell rang. Only when she told me, she had a smile on her face as if this was a good thing, which she knew perfectly well it wasn't. "I heard he's cute now." Darcy was like that. Always finding the good, especially when it came to cute boys. She was sort of an expert. Me? I was definitely behind the times when it came to crushes of any kind. I played with my hair, pulling at the ends, making sure it was still straight since Mom took me to have it done yesterday.

"He could be the cutest boy in town, and it would not make up for how annoying he is."

"People change."

I stared her down. "Not Wolfie."

The bell rang. The room got loud. I stood, frozen. Oh no. I'd definitely have to invite him to my Bat Mitzvah party. That's how Mom was. Perfect. Darcy pulled on my arm.

"Stef, we gotta go," she said.

The bus drivers only wait seven minutes before moving out. I needed to motor. Two guys threw a paper wad down the hall like it was their personal lacrosse field. One nearly ran me over. Paul Watson. Perfect.

"Watch it," I called, my hands up in front of me.

We pushed out the double doors, still an entire walkway from the busses. I dodged and wove and pushed against the wave. Darcy was already on her bus, but mine was always last in line. A mob of kids stood where their bus should have been but wasn't yet. I was just five steps away, thinking that I was going to make it, when Paul Watson zoomed past me. He swerved around the last kid in the way, but then stopped and pushed the kid toward me, making him drop his books and me flail backward, trying not to let my weighty backpack turtle me.

Paul stood at the top of the bus steps, swung on the bar, and pretended to scan for late riders while he stared at me. I heard him say, "What?" to the bus driver. Then "Nope. We're all here." He blew me a kiss as the doors shut me out.

"He really hates you, huh?" The kid sprawled on the pavement brushed off his knees, and I got my first real look at Wolfie, The Returned. When I said he was a pest, I meant like how a tsunami is a little worrisome. There were way too many insults to name over the years, but my least favorite was when he started a water balloon fight at my birthday party. Other people thought it was fun, but I didn't. My big sister, Arly, had straightened my hair for me, and his ridiculous water fight ruined it. Which, by the way, was why I'd decided against a pool party to begin with.

It's not like he worried about what he looked like. I mean, even now his hair was a mop that flopped in front of his eyes. It was dyed blond at the tips and moved every time he spoke, like tiny, little corkscrews. He had on these big black glasses and his typical perma-smirk.

"So the ugly rumors are true, huh?" I said. He shot me a confused look. "You're back."

He smiled. "I *knew* people were talking about me!"

I took out my cell. First things first. I needed to find a way home. Stat.

Just then Wolf's mom pulled up in her old Volvo station wagon, dirt brown colored with mismatching doors. Could this family be any weirder? She rolled down the window and waved. "I'm glad I didn't miss you! Just got off the phone with your mom. I told her I'd get you and take you to shul. As a thank you."

I got dizzy. Surely Mom didn't promise her something from me? Did she?

Text from Mom. One word. Sorry.

Perfect.

* * *

We learned in religious school that Maimonides developed a system for determining the level of tzedakah—charitable donations. The fourth level—the one where you give without being asked—is the sweet spot, the point where the giver's good intentions are not overshadowed by their clumsy egos in order to do a good thing. Mom loved this when I told her about it. She lived this. Which is why every year I helped with the Purim carnival, and this year I was organizing it as part of my mitzvah project.

The car ride to my temple was filled with Wolfie and his mother singing loudly like they were doing Carpool Karaoke or something. His mom almost missed the turn, then took it so hard that I flew across the backseat, even with my seat belt on. Then she slammed on the brakes, leaving me whiplashed and dizzy. Perfect.

"So your mom said you'd help Wolf with his mitzvah project. That OK?"

"Perfect," I answered.

Little did I know just how much time I'd be spending with him. Turns out he hadn't started on anything for his project, so I looped him in with mine, which was to log over two hundred volunteer hours. With very little time left, I was getting in as much volunteering as I could. So Wolfie did also. First, he helped me organize the Purim carnival. Then he helped run it, even talking Talia, a super-shy kindergarten girl who almost never participated in things, into trying every booth at least once. Talia left with a smile on her face. Wolfie left with hamantashen jelly all over him after the pre-K class piled onto him, but he didn't seem to mind. Amazing.

Next was the dance party at the nursing home. Wolfie pretended to know how to waltz. "You dance like a dream," he told Mrs. Wolinsky. He twirled Mrs. Stetson and even did a little dip. The women lit up with his attention, and the men, even old man Johnson whom people called Scrooge behind his back, were impressed by Wolfie's funny dance floor moves. Had I underestimated him? Was he turning into a nice kid after all?

Three weeks to the day from when he moved here and exactly two days from my Bat Mitzvah, I saw him standing by himself by the wall next to the flagpole. Weird. He waved at me. Darcy clutched my arm. "See? He's cute. And I think he liiiikes you!"

I ducked my head but then thought, *Maybe I was wrong about him all along.* Maybe he wasn't so bad. People do change. Don't they? That's when I saw Paul Watson and his friends grouped against the wall leading into the one hundred hall. My mind alert to the danger, I walked slowly up to Wolfie. My first instinct was to warn him. Those guys were trouble. But just as I reached him, Wolfie thrust his hand out and took mine.

I tried to pull away, but then he got down on one knee.

I blushed from head to toe. My heart was going a mile a minute. Wolf was wearing a button-down dress shirt, suspenders, and a bow tie. Like maybe he got dressed up for this thing, whatever this was. He gave me the look. You know *the* look. The *something is about to happen* look.

"I like you, Stef. Will you be my girlfriend?"

Before I could say anything, Paul and his friends burst out of their hiding place, clapped Wolf on the back and high-fived him. One of them had his phone out and was recording. Another snapped pictures. Darcy pulled me away. The last thing I saw was Wolf's crooked smile as the boys surrounded him. "She's so ugly," one of the guys said. "Even you could do better."

Assistant Principal Torrington put his arm around me and ushered me out of the way while Assistant Principal Stevenson started taking names of those involved. I saw them confiscate the phones, and I knew they'd delete the pictures and videos if they hadn't already been shared. But even so, it didn't change the shame that took root inside me.

I sat in the principal's office as they led the boys one at a time into the office next door. They each were forced to sign agreements saying they wouldn't come near me anymore. They were being suspended for bullying, and they lost all their after-school club privileges, something that I'm sure hit Paul pretty hard as he was a big flag football guy.

The whole time I sat there, I hoped not to see him, not to hear his voice, but Mom didn't get there fast enough, and I did hear him.

His voice sounded small and sad. "I didn't mean…"

Principal Snow shut the door, and I couldn't hear the rest of it. What surprised me was that I wanted to listen to what he had to say. I wanted him to be sorry. I wanted more than anything else to have this not to have happened. Why hadn't I walked away? Why had I let him take my hand? Why did I believe this kid was anything but a menace?

Mom appeared in the doorway. I was so grateful it wasn't Dad. "Let's go home," she said.

I didn't want to face her. I didn't want her to know that this kid and Paul and his gang treated me that way. I didn't want anyone to know, especially not my mother, how I was fooled. When I got in the car, I dissolved into tears, even though I worked so hard to keep it all in. I tried not to hear the boy call me ugly. To see them sneer at me. To see them put their arms around Wolfie as he did their awful bidding. I was an idiot.

"Oh, honey," Mom said. We drove home like this, Mom holding my hand; me, leaning against the window, trying not to cry anymore. "I know this doesn't help, but it's been a hard year for Wolf and his mom after, you know, after losing his father."

I hadn't thought about that. Which made me feel like a total jerk.

* * *

Dad let me stay home the next day.

Darcy texted me. Are you ok?

Just when I started to answer her, a text came in from Wolfie. It's not what you think.

I deleted the text and blocked his number.

Mom peeked her head into my room. "I'm going to pick up your grandparents."

My sister and brother came in and sat on my bed.

"You know, Stef, guys are idiots," David said.

Arly nodded. "It's true."

I flopped backward, and she lay next to me.

"And sometimes guys do weird things when they like you."

I sat up straight. Put my hand up like a stop sign. "Don't."

She put her arm around me. "I'm just saying don't think it means he doesn't like you. Because he's kind of…different. And boys, well, they can be so stupid."

"True." David pointed to himself. "I'm a total idiot."

Arly smacked him. He laughed.

"The point is, tomorrow is a big day for you. We want you to enjoy it."

David took out his phone and loaded "The Wizard and I"—Ariana Grande's version. I tried not to let it cheer me up, but when David pretended to hit the high notes, I couldn't help but feel better.

Then I realized he'd be there. Wolf. And I had this weird need to see him. I could picture it. He'd be there trying to get my attention. Trying to face me and own up to what he did. I wanted to have the satisfaction of wiping that perma-smirk off of his face, finally, as I put my hand up and walked away, a group of my friends surrounding me this time. Supporting me. As for Wolf? He'd be the one to feel small.

This was the fantasy that kept me going. That made me go downstairs to greet my grandparents, my aunts and uncles and little cousins. I focused on how he would search for me. Search but not find. Until I was ready to find him.

This thought got me through Shabbat dinner, the services I led afterward, and helped me fall asleep.

As I got ready the next morning for the Torah service, I thought of how I'd have my due.

On the bimah, during the service itself, I continued to think about how good it would feel to get back at him. After services, I stood in the courtyard with my family and friends and ate bagels and tuna salad and black-and-white cookies, but instead of feeling relaxed and proud, I felt focused on one thing—revenge, because I saw at the very edge of the crowd a tuft of curly hair, bleached blond at the ends.

* * *

The party place had put out a red carpet for me—my theme was "starstruck," and I admit, I was slightly awed by how amazing everything looked. My friends huddled in the kids' area where we had a full pasta bar, mini pizzas, black beans and rice, tomato soup, and grilled cheese sandwiches. I was wearing a really awesome dress, a grown-up dress that Arly picked out for me, and I let myself stand up straight as I walked in. We had a photo booth and a light show, but the thing that stood out for me was the dancing and how happy everyone seemed to be. For one second, I forgot about being angry and hurt. I had worked hard for this. I deserved a good time, didn't I?

Arly and David and their friends danced the entire night. My friends from religious school were having a blast. The ones from my middle school joined in. Everything was perfect—until I saw him walk in. Wolfie held his hands in the surrender position as he backed up.

"I'm sorry. I'll leave if you want. I don't want to ruin your night."

I fake laughed. "As if."

He stared at the floor, which gave me time to inspect his outfit. There was nothing that made him stand out. Just a normal blue suit with a white shirt and dark blue tie with a tiny pattern on it. Zigzags of purple and black and light blue and gray and one stripe of pink. "I didn't know," he said.

I didn't ask him what he was referring to. Instead, I thought of his mother, her face hopeful even after her husband died last year of a heart attack. Wolfie too. For the first time, I thought about how hard this all was for him, and I felt bad. With everything he'd gone through, I could see how he could be talked into something. Maybe. But it had still hurt.

"Oh," I said. I looked down. "You weren't with them?" I asked. "You know, doing that on purpose to trick me?"

"No!" His hands flew to his ears. I could tell he was really upset.

"Good. Because it was really a horrible trick."

"The thing is, I wanted to ask you out. I should have known better than to trust those guys."

My eyes met his. I thought of how he was so nice to Talia at the carnival. How he let the kids climb on him with sticky hamantashen hands. How he treated the people at the nursing home. How he lived the tenet of giving before being asked, something I should do more.

He leaned in to whisper to me. "I kicked Paul in the shins before the APs got us."

I laughed. A big sound. So loud I covered my mouth but not before a snort snuck out.

He pointed at me. "You see. This. This is why. You and me. We make a good team."

I heard the familiar sound of the hora. Wolf grabbed a chair. I backed away. "No!"

But soon I was suspended in the air, and everyone was dancing around me. Me. I looked down and saw all of the people I loved. All those who loved me. And this wild-haired boy who was now dancing in the middle of the circle, doing the Russian folk dance where you squat and kick. Pretty impressively too. They lowered me to the ground, and I joined in the circle. On my right was Darcy. On my left, Arly. To her left, David. Mom and Dad were shining brightly as we whirled and whirled and I thought maybe, just maybe, if this moment could keep going, I could float out of here and live in this happiness bubble my whole life.

Then Wolf reached under the table and pulled out a Super Soaker. He made his eyebrows rise, like he was asking permission. Why not? I put my hand out. He gave me his and then grabbed another water gun. Soon more water guns appeared, and the girls shrieked and covered their hair. But me? I chased Wolfie down. Then I squirted him so many times he went down on his knees again and put his hands up to surrender. But he smiled. And it was a real one. No perma-smirk. No one-sided lip lift. A real, honest-to-goodness smile. And making him smile after all he'd been through felt like the best mitzvah of all. Maybe it's true. It was time for me to grow up and grow kinder. Maybe that's what this entire Bat Mitzvah deal was supposed to be about. Who knew?

Arly found me in the bathroom as I dried my hair the best I could. Now wet, the curls sprang to life, some of them sprouting out of their hair-sprayed shellac. Somewhat like Wolfie's.

"I've always loved your hair curly," Arly said. "You should really wear it like that more."

"Maybe."

"So…how do you feel about all of this? You know, the service, the party." She lowered her voice and leaned in closer. "Wolfie?"

I smiled. "Perfect."

The Pocket Watch

Jonathan Rosen

I'm Daniel Lehrman, and my Bar Mitzvah is a disaster.

Okay, it hasn't actually happened yet, but from the way things are going, it's going to be a disaster. You see, some of my friends have had actual famous rock stars perform at their Bar Mitzvahs. Some have even had big-time actors make appearances. And I'm not talking about some D-list ones either. I'm talking about major movie stars. The biggest names from the most popular films. Why, this one girl I know actually had C-3PO and R2-D2 make an appearance at her Star Wars–themed Bat Mitvah.

Needless to say, that's all everyone was talking about at Mark Twain Middle School on Monday.

I'm not sure when the tradition started to make Bar and

Bat Mitzvahs as big a spectacle as weddings, but I wanted in. Unfortunately, as Mom and Dad told me many, many times, things like that required big money, and while there was plenty that my family did have, lots of money wasn't on that list.

So for my Bar Mitzvah, I wasn't going to have celebrities or rock stars, and instead, I was going to have music provided by DJ Mitzvah Mel and the Meshuga Bunch. No, I'm not making that up; that's their real name. I think my dad had a Groupon or something. And as for actors, there was nobody famous going to show at mine either. But on the other hand, I did have my aunt Ashley, who had appeared in a community theater production of *Guys and Dolls* last February. And while you may think that's not a big deal, the *Gravesend Gazette*, our local paper, referred to her as a "standout in an otherwise dreary adaptation."

That newspaper clip is now highlighted and hanging on her refrigerator.

So while I was still excited about my Bar Mitzvah, I have to admit that my expectations have been severely tempered when I compared mine to my classmates'. Not that it's a competition, but yeah, everyone in school acted like it was a competition.

For now, I had to resign myself to the fact that I was going to have the fifteenth best B'nai Mitzvah out of my youth group Kadima chapter. And there were only sixteen of us in there. At least I'm pretty sure that I'd beat out Sarah Lefkowitz's Bat Mitzvah, since her uncle Larry's sleeve caught fire when he was lighting his candle. There were no injuries, but there was a huge scene when the rabbi had to get the fire extinguisher to spray him out. Still, I didn't want to take that victory lap quite yet, since Sarah did manage to play that for laughs for weeks afterward. As a matter of fact, the YouTube video of the incident had racked up a couple of hundred thousand hits. I'd been considering asking Mom if she wouldn't mind doing a pratfall during the mother-son dance so I could post it on social media, but knowing her, she'd never go for it.

So back to my uncool Bar Mitzvah. As of this moment, I have a couple of days left before the big event and nothing at all in the works to make it memorable.

There was a knock at my bedroom door.

I sat up and put my Spider-Man comic down next to me. "Come in."

The door opened, and someone ducked their head in. "How's the Bar Mitzvah boy?"

"Grandpa!" I jumped off the bed and ran to hug him. "I thought you weren't coming until tomorrow."

He kissed my cheek. "I wanted to surprise you!"

I smiled up at him. "Well, you did."

He studied my face. "Is something wrong? You look down."

I frowned. "I don't know. You'll think it's silly."

He placed his hand on my shoulder. "If something is bothering you, I'll never think it's silly."

I thought a moment, stared into his eyes, took a deep breath, and let it out. "Well, it's just that I'm not going to have any celebrities at my Bar Mitzvah."

He snorted. "That's what's bothering you? You're right. That *is* silly."

"You said you wouldn't think that!"

"Yes, but that was before you told me what it was."

I threw my arms up in the air. "Ashley Cohen had C-3PO and R2-D2!"

He shrugged. "So?"

"SO?" My jaw dropped. He was clearly not getting the importance. "Droids, Grandpa! She had real Star Wars droids! That's all everyone talked about for weeks. I mean, even Evan Rothberg had a singer from some eighties group that I never heard of, and everyone was all impressed with that. And nobody even likes Evan Rothberg."

Grandpa sighed and peered down his nose at me.

I threw my head back. "Please don't give me a lecture. Mom and Dad have already done that. I know, I know. These things cost a lot of money."

He smirked. "They do, but that's not what I was going to say." He tousled my hair and then walked to my bed, where he sat on the edge and patted the spot next to him. "Daniel, sit."

I sat beside him. "Okay, go ahead. Tell me that I'm caring about the wrong things like Mom and Dad have already done."

"Should I even speak, or are you going to just have the whole conversation for both of us?"

"Sorry," I muttered. "Go ahead."

He smiled. "When a child becomes Bar or Bat Mitzvahed, they're showing that they are ready to take their place among the Jewish people. To accept responsibility and carry on our traditions."

"I have a feeling that you probably gave the same speech to Mom quite a few times, because she said the same thing."

He laughed. "Well, because it's true. I don't know when Bar Mitzvahs became about who you have instead of what it means, but you need to remember the reason for it." He rubbed my back. "Do you know there have been times when Jews couldn't show any of their identity at all? They used to sneak to do things like praying or observing holidays. There were even kids who risked everything just to have a Bar Mitzvah."

I sighed. "Okay, now I definitely know that you gave that speech to Mom, because it's the EXACT same thing that she said. Maybe it's time to change the script a little?"

He laughed again and gave me a light punch on the arm. "Wise guy!" He rubbed his chin as he stared at me. "You know, I was going to give you something after your Bar Mitzvah, but maybe I'll give it to you now. It might cheer you up a little."

I perked up and arched my eyebrow. "What?"

"Something that's been in our family for a long, long time. I tried to give it to your mother once, but she didn't want the responsibility."

"Responsibility? What is it?"

He reached inside his pants pocket and fished out a small, round, gold object. It was a little smaller than the top of a soda can.

I pointed to it. "What is that?"

He held it up in front of my face. "It's a pocket watch." The corner of his mouth twitched up. "And like I said, it's been in our family for generations."

"Oh..." I stared at it for a moment. "Um, thank you." I reached for it, but he pulled it back.

"You don't seem that enthused by it."

"Grandpa, I am. I, uh, love it. I've just never used one before." I reached for it again, but he pushed my arm down.

Grandpa flipped the cover up and again showed it to me. "It's a very special pocket watch. Your mother spoke to me about possibly giving it to you, and I thought it was a great idea. But it comes with a lot of responsibility."

"Responsibility? Like what do you mean? Not getting it wet? Winding it up every day?"

He smirked. "No, I don't mean that at all. It's just that it's a very special watch."

I narrowed my eyes. "What's so special about it?"

He held it up and smiled. "It's a time machine."

I groaned and winced. "Grandpa, seriously? That's like one of Dad's jokes. I get it. Watch. Time machine. Good one, Grandpa."

Another small laugh. "No, that's not what I meant. I—"

"Dad!" Mom called from the other room. "We're ready to go. Are you coming?"

He stared at me a moment, pressed the pocket watch into my hand, and closed my fist around it. "Here. Why don't you hold this right now, so I don't take it while doing errands with your mother. Put it somewhere safe, and when I get back, I'll show you how to use it."

I squeezed the watch. "Okay, Grandpa."

He wagged his finger at me. "I mean it. Wait until I get back!"

"I said, okay."

"Good boy." He kissed the top of my head. "I'll see you later." He stood and walked out.

I shut the door behind him and examined the watch.

A special pocket watch that's been in the family for generations?

Probably worth a lot of money. Not going to lie, I briefly wondered how much we'd be able to get for it, and if it was too late to get any Star Wars droids.

I flipped it over in my hands.

There was a dial in the center, under which read YEAR. Next to it was a small display square with the current year in it. Under the square was a small button.

"That's weird." I spun the dial, and instead of the time changing, it scrolled through years.

Through the 2000s…

1900s…

1800s…

I furrowed my brow. "What is this thing?"

I looked around the room to see if Mom or Grandpa were playing a trick on me. Nothing looked out of the ordinary, so I opened my door slightly and peered out. The house was quiet.

If this was a trick, they were doing a great job of disguising it.

I turned the pocket watch over again. Nothing seemed unusual about it. Well, except for that little box with the years in it. "All right, I'll bite." Before I could change my mind, I jammed the button down.

Instantly, I was surrounded by orange and red lights streaking by. It felt like I was hurtling through a tunnel, until suddenly, everything came crashing to a stop.

I was no longer in my house. Instead, I was in a small room, watching a kid around my age. He was wearing a kippah and black clothes. The room was packed, and he was surrounded by around thirty older men with long beards. It looked like they were praying.

"They're coming!" a man yelled from the other side of the room.

We all turned to him.

He was standing by a window and looking out. "The Cossacks are coming!"

"Cossacks?" I muttered and thought back to my history classes, where Cossacks invaded Jewish towns for violence. "I'm in Russia?"

Suddenly, the door smashed open and around a dozen men barged in.

Screams echoed throughout. People fled in every direction.

Someone shoved into me, sending the pocket watch flying from my hands, and it went sliding across the floor.

I weaved my way through the mob and snatched it off the ground before diving behind a bench and flipping the pocket watch open. "C'mon, c'mon, get me outta here!" The dial was jammed between two years, and I couldn't tell which ones.

Before I could finish, the bench was yanked to the side.

"NO!" I pressed the button.

The orange and red lights shot out. My stomach churned.

The wind hit my face. The smell of the ocean invaded my senses.

My eyes fluttered open. I was on a ship, along with many other people, crowded by a railing. Before us was the Statue of Liberty.

Someone placed their hand on my shoulder.

I looked up to see a man with a beard smiling at me. "We're in America now. Things will be different here. Better for Jews."

I checked the watch again. The dial was still jammed between two numbers: 1920 and 1921. I forced it up and pressed the button again.

More lights.

I was on a city street. Cars were speeding by. A woman led me by the hand past a diner.

On the door was a sign:

NO DOGS OR JEWS ALLOWED

I stared at it as we walked by. "What?"

Without even looking, I turned the dial and pressed the button.

After the lights whizzed by, I found myself sitting in a room.

Sitting in front of me was an older man. He looked familiar.

He pointed to my hands. "That watch has been in our family for generations, Isaac."

Isaac? "I'm not—" I closed my mouth.

Wait a second…

I peered around the man to stare at the mirror. This face, I recognized. I had seen it in many pictures before. The Isaac he was talking to was my grandfather.

I was in his body!

The man in front of me had to be my great-grandfather. "You are the first in our family to freely have a Bar Mitzvah out in the open. No fear of persecution. It is a momentous occasion." He smiled and closed my fist around the pocket watch, in the same way Grandpa had done earlier. "Remember, you are part of a chain of the Jewish people. Don't be the link that breaks."

I nodded but couldn't speak. The words were trapped in my throat.

He walked out, and I looked down at the pocket watch in my hands.

The dial turned easily now, and I set it back to my year and pressed the button.

I was back in my room, on my bed.

Unfortunately, there was a very disapproving face staring down at me.

Grandpa was standing there with his arms crossed. "Didn't I tell you not to touch the watch until I showed you how it worked?"

"Grandpa!" I rushed over and hugged him. "I'm sorry, I just—"

He placed his hand under my chin and lifted my head until my eyes met his. "I said to wait because the watch isn't a toy."

I looked away. "I know. I didn't mean to. It's just that…"

"I know." The seriousness from his face left and a warm glow took its place. "Thankfully, there was no harm done. But now that you've seen what it can do, you need to be more careful in the future. The watch isn't exactly a time machine like you think. With this, you slide into the body of someone who experienced history and take over for them for as long as you're there." He gave a slight nod. "Our family are sort of observers of history. We record it and document it. There are others like us, but not many. It is our duty to make sure this doesn't fall into the wrong hands." He stared into my eyes. "That could be very dangerous. So, you see, you really need to act responsibly." He placed his hand on my shoulder. "Like I said before, it's our family's obligation to care for it."

"How did this start, Grandpa? Who gave this to us? How did—"

He held his hand up. "Those are stories for another day. For now, all you need to know is what a tremendous responsibility this is that I'm giving you. It's not a toy or something for self-gain. It's a huge undertaking."

I hugged him again. "I understand, Grandpa! And I'll be careful with it. I promise. This is the best Bar Mitzvah gift ever."

He tousled my hair and took the watch from me. "Let me hold this until the ceremony is over. That way, you concentrate on your Bar Mitzvah and won't get distracted by the watch. When it is over, you and I will sit together, and I'll show you precisely how to use it."

I nodded. "Okay, Grandpa." I thought a moment. "Grandpa, you've never been tempted to use it for anything other than observing?"

He smiled. "Of course I've been tempted, but I've only let myself veer from our responsibility a couple of times for special occasions."

My eyes widened. "What did you do?"

He winked at me. "More stories for another day. In the meantime, all you need to remember is, a Bar Mitzvah is not about the gifts or who appears or how big the party is. It's about…"

* * *

"Becoming part of the Jewish community. Preserving tradition. Not being the link that breaks the chain. This is what's important. There will always be those who seek to destroy us, not wanting us to continue as a people, but I'm going to do my best to keep our traditions going forward and pass them on to the next generation," I said to all the guests. The same words that Grandpa had told me, and his father had told him, and who knows how many generations before that had told their children.

Everyone stood and applauded, and I smiled out at Mom, Dad, and Grandpa.

I ran to my seat between Mom and Grandpa. My family all hugged me.

"So proud of you!" Mom and Dad said in unison.

Grandpa squeezed me tight.

I hugged him back. "You were right, Grandpa. I didn't need anything else. I'm just happy everyone was with me."

He kissed my cheek. "You're a good boy, Daniel."

DJ Mitzvah Mel came out onstage.

He cleared his throat and looked out at the sea of people in the hall. "Thank you. But before we finish, we do have one more speech.

A special guest who just wanted to say a few words."

My brow furrowed. I was supposed to have been the last speech. I turned to Mom. "Who else is speaking?"

Mom smiled at me. "It wasn't me." She motioned to Grandpa. "He has a surprise for you."

A tall, thin man, with a short, black beard walked out. He was dressed in a black suit. He looked out, removed his stovepipe hat, and placed it in front of him on the dais before leaning forward. "A half score and three years ago, Daniel Lehrman was born…"

Everyone laughed.

I leaned over and whispered to Grandpa. "You got a Lincoln impersonator for my Bar Mitzvah?"

Grandpa looked into my eyes and smiled. "*Impersonator?*"

The realization of his words hit me. "You mean…" I pointed to Lincoln. "He's—"

Grandpa nodded.

My jaw dropped. "Grandpa, whatever happened to only using the watch for observing?"

He gave a sheepish grin. "Well, I did say I've made exceptions for special occasions, and since when isn't my grandson's Bar Mitzvah a special occasion?" He shrugged. "And besides, Lincoln owed me a favor."

I turned back to Lincoln and watched him finish giving his speech, but all I could think was, *This is the best Bar Mitzvah ever!*

Grandma Merle's Last Wish

Melissa Roske

I was at the Starlight Diner, scraping mayo off my BLT, when my mom dropped the Bat Mitzvah bomb. "I know it's a lot to ask," she said as she signaled to the waiter for more coffee, "but it would mean the world to Grandma Merle. You know, before she..." Mom searched for the right word. "*Goes.*"

Mom didn't mean go to the Whispering Pines Retirement Village, where Grandma Merle spends her winters, playing canasta and gossiping with her friends. She meant something more permanent, like *die*. My grandma's been planning her "final farewell" for years. The last time my family went to visit her in Florida—two years ago, over spring break—Grandma Merle asked my sister, Lily, and me to go through her jewelry box and choose one piece each. *A little something to remember me by*, she said. *Go on… Take something!*

It felt wrong to accept Grandma Merle's jewelry while she was still alive, so I grabbed the first thing I saw: an ugly pair of rhinestone clip-ons, which I knew I'd never wear. Lily, who's sixteen and never says no to free *anything*, inspected every ring, brooch, and necklace until she settled on a gold butterfly pin with tiny rubies glistening on its wings. She wore it pinned to her bathing suit for the rest of the trip, making me wonder whether I should've taken something better than cheap earrings.

My mind flew back to Grandma Merle's weird request. Why would she want me to have a Bat Mitzvah? Bat Mitzvahs are for kids who go to Hebrew school and get dragged to temple by their parents on the High Holy Days. The most Jewish thing I've ever done is decorate our Hanukkah bush and eat bagels and lox for brunch. That hardly counts. Doesn't Grandma Merle know this?

I asked my mom for a better explanation. One that made sense.

"Many people turn to religion as they get older," Mom said. "It gives them a sense of comfort. You know, for when their time comes."

I knew which "time" my mom meant.

"It wouldn't have to be anything fancy," she continued, "just a small private ceremony in the rabbi's study. You wouldn't even have to learn Hebrew—Grandma Merle checked. You'd read your Torah portion in English. The blessings too. Afterward, we can have a nice lunch somewhere. Come on, Bella…what do you say?"

I'd say my mom was losing it. There was no way I was having a

Bat Mitzvah. It was crazy. Not just crazy but run-down-the-block-in-your-underwear crazy. "Why can't Lily do it?" I asked, knowing my sister was the better choice. "And don't say she's too old, because Rachel's mom had one last year and she's at least *forty*!"

Mom coughed into her napkin. "I hear what you're saying, honey, but your sister is too busy for a Bat Mitzvah. She's got a huge academic workload, plus college applications and ballet. Besides, Grandma Merle asked specifically for you."

"She *did*?"

My mom nodded.

"Why? I've met her, like, ten times in my life!"

Mom put down her coffee cup. "I know you and your grandma aren't close, which is probably my fault. But I think she regrets not knowing you better. Now that she's getting on in years, she doesn't want to miss the opportunity."

"Can't I just go visit her in Florida?" I asked. "That's a lot easier than having a Bat Mitzvah!"

"I don't disagree with you, but Grandma Merle has been very good to us. I also know she's lonely. Sure, she has friends in Boca, and she has a few here, in New York. But watching you get Bat Mitzvahed would be the highlight of her life."

"Did she say that?"

"Not exactly," Mom admitted. "Her exact words were: 'This is my last wish.'"

Last wish? Talk about a guilt trip!

"I'll think about it," I said, wondering what happens to kids who don't grant their grandmother's last wishes, "but I'm not making any promises."

That night, Mom stopped by my room. She sat down on the edge of my bed. "Daddy and I were talking," she said, "and I realize I might have been pressuring you. The decision to have a Bat Mitzvah is a big one—and it's not mine to make."

I sat up, fast. "You mean it?"

Mom leaned over and kissed the top of my head. "You're officially off the hook."

Whew!

But then, as I was drifting off to sleep, I started to think about what Mom had said at lunch:

Grandma Merle has been very good to us.

She's lonely.

Watching you get Bat Mitzvahed would be the highlight of her life.

This is her last wish.

How could I say no to that?

I couldn't.

* * *

The following week, Mom took me to Temple Beth Shalom to meet with Grandma Merle's rabbi. I'd never been face-to-face with a rabbi before, and Rabbi Goodman caught me gawking.

"You thought I'd be old and wrinkly, with a long, gray beard," she said, inviting me into her study. "Am I right?"

I nodded, feeling my face burn. "I'm sorry," I said.

"Don't be. Lots of people—Jews and non-Jews alike—make all kinds of assumptions about rabbis. What they should look like, who they should be..." Rabbi Goodman made air quotes around the *should*s. "Assumptions are made about B'nai Mitzvahs too. Specifically, who 'should' have one." She eyed me carefully. "I'm guessing you might feel this way."

Whoa. Rabbi Goodman was a mind reader! Considering I was barely Jewish, it felt wrong to have a Bat Mitzvah. Like I didn't deserve one. "It was my grandma's idea," I admitted. "But I guess you know that."

"I do," Rabbi Goodman said with a smile. "Tell me more."

I felt myself relax as Rabbi G—that's what she told me to call her—listened to my feelings about Grandma Merle's crazy request (I left out the word "crazy," because I didn't want to be disrespectful). I also told her how nervous I was. This was all new to me, and I was scared I'd mess up.

Rabbi G got up from behind her desk and sat down in the chair next to mine. Her eyes were kind. "I understand what you're saying, Bella, but remember...Temple Beth Shalom welcomes everyone, and this won't be a traditional Bat Mitzvah. We'll have the ceremony here, in my study, and your Torah and haftarah portions will be in English. The Hebrew blessings will be transliterated—that means, spelled out phonetically. That way, you can say the words even if you don't know Hebrew. The important thing is that you take something positive away from this experience—and have fun."

Fun? The thought hadn't crossed my mind. Until now.

"The ceremony will take place on the morning of Saturday, June twenty-sixth," Rabbi G was saying, counting off three months on her fingers, "so this doesn't give us much time. But if you work hard and show up for our weekly tutoring sessions, you'll be well prepared."

I gave Rabbi G my promise to work hard and show up, leaving her study with three books in my backpack: *Understanding Judaism*, which the rabbi said would help me learn the basics; *Surviving Your Bar/Bat Mitzvah*, which was written by one of her friends from rabbinical school; and a novel, *My Basmati Bat Mitzvah*, "for pleasure reading."

The following week, Rabbi G showed me my Torah portion. She explained that the Torah is cyclical, meaning that each portion is scheduled to be read on a specific day. "In other words," she said, "you don't get to choose."

When I got home, I realized why Rabbi G told me about not getting to choose. My portion, Parashah Balak, was about a talking donkey.

At the next tutoring session, I was given my haftarah—a selection from one of the biblical books of the prophets, which is read after the Torah portion—and the week after that, the blessings. When I told Rabbi G there was no way I'd learn everything by the end of June, she reminded me that Rome wasn't built in a day.

I guess I was Rome.

At the end of May, five weeks before my Bat Mitzvah, Grandma Merle flew back to New York. She invited me over to her apartment, on the Upper West Side, for Sunday brunch. *Just the two of us.*

"I got the good bagels," she said as soon as I walked in. "From Zabar's." She stood back to admire me. "You've grown so much, bubbeleh. You're taller than I am!"

We both laughed because that wasn't hard. My grandma is tiny, five feet tall at the *most*. "Did you know that bubbeleh means 'little grandmother' in Yiddish?" Grandma Merle said as she led me into the kitchen. "Pretty funny, huh?"

"I didn't know you speak Yiddish."

"I don't," she admitted, passing me the bagels. "I've been taking Yiddish classes at the Jewish Community Center, in Boca. My parents spoke it, but they never taught me. I figured it was high time I learned. You know, before I—"

I held my breath, waiting for Grandma Merle to say "go," or "meet my maker." Instead, she spread some egg salad on her bagel and took a big bite. "How's the Bat Mitzvah studying coming along?" she asked between mouthfuls. "Are you ready for the big day?"

I wasn't sure how to answer that. I'd been working with Rabbi G on my Torah and haftarah portions, and I knew the blessings by heart. I also knew tons more about Judaism than when I'd started. Still, I felt scared. I shared my worries with my grandmother.

"You'll be fine, sweetheart," she said, reaching for my hand. "Better than fine. You'll be fabulous!"

"How do you know?" I wiped a blob of egg salad off my chin.

"Because *you're* fabulous. Everybody knows that."

"They do?"

"Sure." Grandma Merle put down her bagel. "Remember when you visited me in Florida, and I asked you and your sister to go through my jewelry box?"

I nodded.

"Well, I noticed that you didn't choose anything valuable—just those old rhinestone earrings." She leaned in closer. "I admired that about you, Bella. It showed your character—that you're not a taker. Now, I'm not saying anything negative about your sister. Lily is a lovely girl. But you're…*special*."

Suddenly, I realized why my grandma wanted me to have a Bat Mitzvah. It wasn't because she was trying to find comfort in religion before she died, or even that she wanted to get to know me better. She wanted me to get to know *her*.

* * *

Over the next few weeks, I studied for my Bat Mitzvah and hung out with Grandma Merle. We got strawberry milkshakes at Emack & Bolio's, visited the Museum of Natural History, and went to Lincoln Center to hear the New York Philharmonic. She even got us tickets for *Fiddler on the Roof*—in Yiddish. "Don't worry," Grandma Merle said, squeezing my arm as we entered the theater. "The English translation will be projected onto a big screen. It'll be great!"

My grandma was right. As I watched the story of the Russian milkman and his daughters unfold, I forgot that I didn't understand Yiddish. I'm pretty sure Grandma Merle was trying to make a point, but I didn't know what it was—until the day of my Bat Mitzvah.

I'd just finished my Torah portion, when Rabbi G gave me the nod to start the blessing. As I was reading, I realized it didn't matter that I didn't understand Hebrew—or that I ate BLT sandwiches and decorated a Hanukkah bush. I was doing something special for Grandma Merle, just as she'd done so many special things for me.

I looked up from my prayer book and smiled at my grandma before reciting the last two lines of the blessing.

Blessed are You, Adonai our G-d, Sovereign of the universe,

who has given us a Torah of truth, implanting within us eternal life.

I wish I could give eternal life to Grandma Merle, to stop her from worrying about her "final farewell." But I did grant her last wish, even though there was nothing "last" about it.

To me, it was just the beginning.

A Funny Thing Happened on the Way to the Bimah

Laura Shovan

I, Dani Karet, was in a pickle.

Not an actual pickle. Do not remind me of the great sixth-grade Halloween fiasco. Take my advice. If your friends want to trick-or-treat dressed as parts of a fast-food burger—hold the cheese—*run away*. No snack-sized candy is worth that level of embarrassment.

No.

This was a metaphorical pickle.

"Your meeting with Rabbi Birnbaum is tomorrow," Mom said after breakfast, as I bundled up in a coat, gloves, hat, and scarf. "Last check-in before the big day."

"Tomorrow?" I gulped.

"I can't believe it's so close," Mom gushed. She put her hands on my shoulders and stood back to look at me.

It's a wonder she knew who I was under all my layers of goose down and wool.

"My little girl, a Bat Mitzvah!" Mom pulled me close and squeezed.

"Ugh, Mom. I'm steaming hot."

"Go. Go." Mom shooed me out of the house. "It's tech week. I've got to get your brother to school and hurry over to the theater. Galit will be here when you get home."

Tech week was the worst. Mom spent more time at the university with her drama students than she did with me, my older sister Galit, or our little brother Noah.

Whose idea was it to schedule my Bat Mitzvah the weekend after her winter show? Not mine. It wasn't as if I could change my birthday.

I trudged outside. There'd been a cold snap the last few days, but my best friend, Astrid Pease, and I were walking to school anyway. The ten-minute trek was our time to talk without adults around.

Astrid was at the corner, jumping up and down to stay warm.

Astrid isn't Jewish. How was I going to explain that I was a nervous wreck? The kind of feeling you get backstage on opening night, having rehearsed for months and lived through a disastrous dress rehearsal, when it's now or never, the curtain's finally opening and...

I had to stop thinking about it before I lost my Cheerios all over the sidewalk.

"What's with the frown?" Astrid asked as I caught up to her.

"How do you know I'm frowning?" I waved a mitten in front of my yarn-wrapped face. "I look like an unshorn sheep."

"It's your eyes." Astrid peered into my face. "Let me guess. Bat Mitzvah stress plus tech week equals one miserable Dani."

She put an arm around my shoulders. I allowed the PDA because I was freezing.

"Take it from your best friend, you have nothing to stress about. You've been studying for months. If your Bat Mitzvah were a test, you'd ace it! What's to worry?"

I pulled my scarf down, letting a cloudy breath escape. "What's to worry? My last meeting with the rabbi is tomorrow, and I still haven't started my speech."

To be honest, I had plenty of things to say about my d'var Torah, the short speech I was supposed to give after chanting my Torah portion.

Things like:

I can't do this!

It's too stressful.

My writing stinks.

If twenty rabbis can't agree on the meaning of this word, who am I to offer my opinion?

"Didn't you say it only has to be five minutes?" Astrid asked.

"Three to five," I said. "The longest three to five minutes of my life."

"Longer than the time when you got stuck in the pickle costume?"

"We agreed to never speak of that!"

Astrid smiled. "You've got this, Dani. You have your lines memorized. In Hebrew. You don't even speak Hebrew!"

Studying my Torah portion wasn't exactly like running lines for the middle school production of *The Little Mermaid*, but I let it slide.

Astrid stopped in the middle of the sidewalk and faced me. For someone who wore her hair in babyish pigtails ("All the K-Pop idols are wearing them," Astrid had explained), my best friend could look very serious.

She put her hands on my shoulders. What was it with people putting their hands on my shoulders today? Was I hunching?

"I believe in you," Astrid said.

I shrugged her off.

My high-tops felt heavier with every step, but the cold kept me moving.

"I wish I shared your confidence. Remember when our class performed scenes from *Wind in the Willows* for the PTA in fourth grade? The only dialogue I could remember was Mr. Toad saying, 'Toot! Toot!' It wasn't even my line."

"You're the only one who remembers that." Astrid twirled a blond pigtail around her gloved finger, a sure sign she was lying. "So, what are you going to do?"

Good question. And the answer that popped out of my mouth surprised me.

"I'm going to get out of it. Somehow, someway."

"Or you could ask people for advice," Astrid said. "I've never been to a Bat Mitzvah, so I'm not the right person to ask, but…" She gave me a sideways glance.

Which meant I was about to get a whole lot of advice.

"What about throwing in some choreo?" Astrid suggested. "If you bust some dance moves, it'll help drive home your point."

"Astrid, my Torah portion tells the story of the Ten Plagues."

"The what?"

"You know, when the Jews were slaves in Egypt, and Moses told Pharaoh, 'Let my people go,' only he wouldn't, so G-d unleashed the Ten Plagues."

Astrid still looked confused, so I kept going. "Blood, frogs, lice, flies, pestilence, boils, hail, locusts, darkness, and the killing of the firstborn," I recited. I would've counted them off on my fingers, but my fingers were wrapped in three layers of mittens.

"Astrid, how am I supposed to do choreo for lice?"

Astrid pulled a shoulder up to her ear and pretended to pick something out of her hair. Right, left, right, left. She popped her hips and flipped her pigtails with each move.

"Only you could make picking bugs out of your hair look cute," I grumbled.

"Trust me. It'll work," Astrid argued. "It's like miming the story, helping your audience follow along."

"Fine," I said. "But lice is an easy one. Got any dance moves for boils?"

"Hey, Pease and Karet. Wait up!"

We turned to see our lunch buddy, Newman R. Frye, a.k.a. Nerf, coming up the sidewalk. His puffy gray jacket was so large, his hat, scarf, and gloves so all-encompassing, I wouldn't have recognized Nerf if it weren't for his size. He'd entered sixth grade as one of the smallest kids in our class. Now he towered over most of our teachers.

Astrid and I gave each other a look, as we did every time Nerf called us "Pease and Karet." I wanted to ask Nerf to stop referring to us as a plate of vegetables. Astrid argued it was worth it if we wanted to keep calling him Nerf instead of Newman.

"I'm giving Dani advice on her Bat Mitzvah," Astrid said. She stopped for a quick dance break that ended with her waving a finger in front of my face.

"Two weeks. I cannot wait," Nerf said. "My mom's letting me wear my brother's recital tux to the party." He spun on one loafered foot. "Have I mentioned I look good in a tux?"

"The party's not the problem," Astrid said. "It's the ceremony."

"I'm fine with reading from the scroll," I told Nerf. "But I also have to give a speech about it."

I was supposed to share my thoughts on Va'era, my Torah portion, something the most learned minds of our community had been discussing for hundreds of years. No wonder I was stressing out! What was the point?

I aimed my toe at a stone, intending to kick it into the grass. Of course, I misfired, tripped, and would have landed on my tuchus if

Nerf hadn't caught my elbow and pulled me back toward the school's front entrance.

"The point of what?" Nerf said.

Whoops. Talking out loud again.

"The point of making a speech at my Bat Mitzvah. I have to read it to my rabbi tomorrow. And I haven't written one word," I moaned.

Astrid opened the school's front doors. We stepped into the blessed heat and walked to our lockers.

Nerf said, "How about throwing in some song lyrics? You know, rewrite something that's getting airplay, make it all Biblical."

"You want me to write a pop parody? Do I look like Weird Al Yankovic to you?"

To be fair, with my brown curly hair and pointy chin, I could have been Weird Al's long-lost, beardless second cousin.

Nerf nodded. "Maybe you're right. My uncle's a lawyer for a record company. His firm had this big trial 'cause someone used song lyrics without the artist's permission. Not cool."

I felt my eyes bug out. "I'm only twelve. I'm too young to get sued. Besides, the only song lyrics I know are from Sondheim musicals."

"Who now?" Nerf asked.

"Oh no," Astrid said. "Now you've done it. We're about to get a lecture on…"

She said it with me: "The greatest living composer and lyricist Broadway has ever known."

"I repeat: Who?" Nerf handed Astrid the end of his scarf. She pulled. He spun. Finally, I could see his face.

It was almost homeroom, so I gave Nerf the short version. "My mom's a professor at the community college. She doesn't just teach musical theater. She lives it. We all live it, especially when her students are putting on show," I explained as we each grabbed our textbooks. "I couldn't tell you what's on the radio, but I know every song in *A Funny Thing Happened on the Way to the Forum*."

"Should I even ask?" Nerf asked.

"It's the show Dr. Karet's students are staging right now." Astrid swept her arm in front of her as if imagining the scene. "Think ancient Rome. Think people singing and dancing in togas."

I sighed. Why couldn't I have the speaking powers of Pseudolus, the main character in *Forum*? Pseudolus is a slave in ancient Rome, doing everything he can think of to earn his freedom. He gives people potions, pretends to be someone else, stages a fake funeral—everything short of the Ten Plagues.

Pseudolus is hilarious. His witty comments and quick thinking are at the heart of the play, and the audience loves him.

When *I* was stressed out, I could barely manage a squeak.

I sat through my morning classes, wondering how I could get out of tomorrow's meeting. Fall off the rope in PE and get a concussion? Eat the school's fish tacos and land myself with a case of food poisoning? Mix the wrong chemicals in science and cause a minor explosion?

Those things might buy me sympathy, and possibly a suspension, but there was no getting out of my Bat Mitzvah.

The truth was, I didn't really want to get out of it. I'd spent six months studying with my Torah tutor and listening to recordings of our cantor singing the parashah. If I messed up, I knew the cantor and Rabbi Birnbaum would be there to back me up. The speech was the one part of the Bat Mitzvah ceremony when no one would be there to fix my mistakes. Or shake people's shoulders if they started to snooze.

I wished I could read my Torah portion and be done. Rabbi Birnbaum could give the sermon. No one would notice. Especially not school friends like Astrid and Nerf, who weren't Jewish. I was fairly sure all they cared about was the party after the ceremony. Astrid had already given me a list of K-pop tunes to hand to the DJ.

In French class, I ignored Madame Johnson's verb conjugations and doodled a guy in a toga.

"Pseudolus," I whispered to the tubby, balding figure on my paper. "What can I borrow from your bag of tricks?"

Hmm. Maybe I could dress my spotlight-loving little brother, Noah, in a suit identical to the one I was wearing for the ceremony—gray with pink pinstripes. It was a trick worthy of Pseudolus. Noah would give the speech for me. Stick a Weird Al wig on him, and no one would know the difference.

Except that Noah was at least three inches shorter than me. If only I had a quick-grow potion I could feed him. Better yet, I could teach Noah to walk in Mom's high heels.

At lunch, I zombied my way into the cafeteria, my mind still plotting how to get out of tomorrow's meeting.

Astrid noticed how distracted I was. She pointed her chopsticks at me as she slurped udon noodles out of her thermos. "Nerf and I were talking in chorus about which would be better for your d'var Torah, K-pop choreo or a song parody."

"Not this again," I groaned.

Nerf strode up to our table, waving his arms. "I thought we agreed, Pease. No swaying the judge before the competition."

I was dumbfounded. "Competition?"

Astrid stood up and put on her best girl-group pose.

Nerf grabbed a plastic fork, holding it in front of his mouth like a microphone.

Astrid stared Nerf down.

Nerf glared back.

"It's a perform-off." Astrid popped a hip and shifted into a new pose. "Thirty seconds each to convince you who's got the best advice for your speech."

Nerf did some vocal warm-ups into his fork. Loudly. "Then we each get a fifteen-second rebuttal. Can you time us, Dani?"

"That's okay, you guys. I appreciate it, but..."

They did rock, paper, scissors to see who would go first. Nerf won.

Nerf has an amazing voice. He sings at his church and always gets solos at the Dickinson Middle School music night. But no one expected him to start belting in the middle of lunch.

The entire seventh grade froze, with half-chewed fish tacos in their gaping mouths, and stared at our table.

Thirty seconds later, Nerf dropped his fork.

I mean, his mic.

"That's how you get a crowd's attention," Nerf bragged, bowing to the rapt tables of seventh graders.

"And this is how you keep it," Astrid said. Before I could stop her, Astrid stepped onto our table's bench seat. She would've kept going if the lunch monitor hadn't arrived and escorted a protesting Astrid out of the cafeteria.

"You can't stop the beat!" she screamed as they dragged her away, quoting from *Hairspray*, one of our favorite non-Sondheim musicals.

"So?" Nerf asked. "I win by default, right?"

I felt like the wilting banana in my lunch bag. My appetite was gone. "I cannot wait for this day to be over."

* * *

"Mom!" I screeched as I dropped my backpack by our front door.

"At the theater," came my older sister's voice from the kitchen.

I'd been hoping to laugh away my anxiety by describing my awful day in vivid yet comical detail to Mom. If anyone could appreciate drama, it was my mother.

Instead, I was stuck with the fifteen-year-old queen of the debate scene.

People who didn't know any better thought my sister, Galit, was average. She was regular height. Her hair was brown, with the average amount of waviness (which was not fair, in my opinion). Galit's nose wasn't too big or too small. Her voice was honey sweet.

Until you started a quarrel, a disagreement, a dispute. And then the full Galit gale of words hit you with a barrage of logic no human adolescent could overcome.

I groaned and walked into the kitchen.

"What's wrong, Pickle?" Galit asked, looking up from whatever legal tome she was studying. This year's debate topic was "the sale of human organs should be legalized." Ew.

"Don't call me Pickle. How is anyone going to forget the great sixth-grade Halloween fiasco if you keep calling me Pickle?"

"Make a compelling argument and I'll consider it," Galit countered.

"I've made a decision," I declared as I rummaged in the cupboards for a snack. "I'm going to figure out how to get out of my d'var Torah."

"Get out of it?" Galit lowered her glasses, so she could give me a disapproving stare. "It's your chance to shine. To say what you think. Why memorize a Torah portion if you're not going to share your ideas about it?"

She picked up a celery stick and waved it at me. "In fact," she said with an emphatic crunch, "that's the whole point."

"But it's the Ten Plagues," I reminded her. "What could I possibly add? We tell that story every year at Passover."

Galit narrowed her eyes at me and stood up. She began to pace, back and forth, across the kitchen.

I, Dani Karet, was about to be argued at.

"I'll help you." Galit pounded her palm with her fist.

"You will? That would be amazing. Astrid and Nerf want me to sing and dance, but that's not me. Keep it simple, right?"

Galit took a rubber band off her wrist, pulling her hair into a severe bun.

I backed away. My sister followed.

"Forget it." I grabbed a box of graham crackers and ran from the kitchen. "I'll figure it out myself."

"Wait!"

Somehow, Galit was standing in front of me, blocking my path. I skidded to halt.

I tried to dive around her, but Galit weaved left. I dodged to the right, but she was too fast. She was like a squirrel. And I was her nut.

"I have so much to teach you," Galit said. "At least let me give you my top ten tips for public speaking."

"Three tips, max, and then I'm outta here."

"Number one." Galit marched to the stairs and stood two steps above me. She still hadn't forgiven me for getting taller than her over the summer.

I tried to push past her and escape to our (sigh) shared bedroom, but Galit stepped back and held a finger up to my face.

"Research. Months of research. You will read, highlight, and annotate every case and precedent in order to form a solid argument." She looked at me quizzically. "When is the competition?"

Galit was growing scarier by the moment. I had no doubt that someday my sister would reach her goal. She'd be a Supreme Court justice like her hero, Ruth Bader Ginsburg.

"You mean my Bat Mitzvah?!" I was getting hysterical. "In two weeks. But I have to read my speech to Rabbi Birnbaum tomorrow."

"Okay. Don't panic." Galit blew out three quick breaths. "Twenty-four hours. That's not so bad. If you don't sleep, how many rabbinical commentaries can you review in twenty-four hours?"

My eyes crossed just thinking about it.

I knew I should have eaten fish tacos for lunch. If I barfed, Mom would insist I stay in bed tomorrow.

No school.

No meeting.

No speech.

I clutched the graham crackers to my chest like a shield and stepped forward. Galit moved with me, waving two fingers.

"Oh no you don't. I promised three tips. Number two. Confidence!"

"Confidence?" I echoed weakly.

"Don't approach the bimah with your head down." Galit pushed my shoulders back. "You look like a walking question mark. But you, Dani Karet, are an exclamation point! Repeat after me: I am an exclamation point."

"I am an exclamation point," I mumbled. "Can I go now?"

Galit put up three fingers. "Tip three. Speak quickly."

"Quickly?"

I cowered as my sister leaned over me. Once again, she pounded a fist on her open palm.

"The precedent for this speech is that it must be three to five minutes. Do you assent or deny?"

"I assent! I assent! Just don't hit me!"

"To get as much information across as you can, you must speak quickly, like this."

Galit opened her mouth. Out poured a torrent of words. They spewed from Galit's lips like a marauding flock of crows, ready to peck her debate opponents to pieces.

I was impressed. I didn't understand a word of it.

"Well?" Galit asked.

"I'd rather sing a Ten Plagues medley," I said, "with choreo."

Galit shrugged. She plucked a sleeve of graham crackers out of the box. "Mind if I eat these?"

"As long as you don't talk them to death first," I said under my breath.

* * *

I explained my dilemma to Dad as he made dinner. Mom was still at the theater.

"My Bat Mitzvah speech is a disaster. Which is saying a lot because I haven't even started it yet."

Dad turned and hugged me.

"Everyone I asked for advice has a different idea," I complained into Dad's apron-covered middle.

"I've got the perfect solution," he said.

"You do?"

"This calls for a spreadsheet."

"A spreadsheet?" I looked up at him, incredulous.

Dad's eyes sparkled, as they always did when his analytical brain was working on a problem. "A spreadsheet is the perfect tool for looking at the plusses and minuses of multiple angles."

"It's a speech, Dad. Not a math test."

But he was on a roll. "We'll make a column for each person you asked for advice. Underneath that, the advice given. Then we will break down the positives and negatives of each approach. Oh," he said, waving salad tongs in the air. "Let's color code the different options. That will make it fun! Get your homework done, and we'll start on it after dinner."

My head was spinning again.

"Maybe I should go straight to bed. I'm feeling a little sick." I attempted a feeble cough. "Don't want to give the rabbi a cold." I sniffled loudly. "I should probably skip the meeting."

"Nonsense," Dad said. "Once everything is laid out in columns and rows, you'll know what to do."

* * *

After dinner, Noah illegally stuck his toes into the bedroom I shared with Galit. He wiggled them at me, just to be annoying.

"You didn't ask *me* for advice on your speech," Noah said.

I patted the bed. Noah skipped across the carpet and sat down beside me.

"How come your side is so messy and Galit's is so neat?"

I glared at him and ignored the question. "I'm sorry I didn't ask you. But I've gotten so much advice today, I don't know whether to sing, or dance, or speed-talk, or what! It doesn't help that I have to talk about one of the most famous stories in the Torah. What could I possibly add?"

"Jokes. Everyone likes jokes."

"Okay...you got one I can use?" I was that desperate.

Noah bounced up and down on my bed. "I've got a good one! What do you call a dinosaur fart?"

I slapped my palm to my forehead. My Torah portion was about the Jews breaking out of slavery. Not about breaking wind.

"A blast from the past!" My brother doubled over, laughing to himself. He fell sideways, kicking his feet.

When Noah stopped laughing, he said, "I have better advice than that though."

"Better than a farting dinosaur?"

Noah nodded. "I have 'get out of school' advice."

I looked at my brother with new respect. "That's more like it. Hit me."

He did.

"Ouch! I didn't mean literally, you numbskull."

"It's cold out," Noah said.

"Yeah. That happens in January."

"Cold enough to snow." Noah wiggled his eyebrows. "All we have to do is wear our pajamas inside out, flush three ice cubes down the toilet, and spin around thirteen times." He sat back and crossed his arms over his chest. "Guaranteed snow day."

I stood up and looked out my window. Stars shone in a cloudless night sky.

"It can't hurt," I said with a sigh. "You get the ice cubes. I'll change into pajamas."

"Before I go downstairs, can I borrow a pen?" Noah asked. "I saw a make-your-own-prank video on YouTube and I want to try it."

"Anything for you. If this snow day stuff works, I'll owe you for a miracle."

I gave his forehead a big smooch. Noah wiped the kiss off and grabbed a pen off my desk.

* * *

Noah and I had already put on our PJs (inside out *and* backward) and flushed a bowl full of ice cubes down the toilet. We had taken over the family room, pushed furniture out of the way, and were starting our series of thirteen spins to bring on a blizzard when

Mom walked in.

She wore her black *I Can't, It's Tech Week* T-shirt. Her arms were splattered with paint. Her face was scowling.

"Whoa!" Mom leaned against a wall for support. "I've been staging pratfalls all night. And don't get me started on togas. Those things are a tripping hazard. What in the world are you two up to?"

"Can't stop, Mom!" Noah said. "We have to spin exactly thirteen times, or the snow won't come."

"Dani?" Mom asked.

"Nine, ten, eleven," I counted, tottering from the spinning.

"What's going on with the toilet?!" Galit shouted from upstairs. "Dad!"

Dad got up from his laptop, said a quick hello to Mom, and pounded up the stairs.

Whoops. Too many ice cubes.

"Thirteen." I fell onto the couch. "Noah and I are making it snow."

Mom crossed her arms, so her T-shirt read *I Can't*.

"This wouldn't have anything to do with your meeting tomorrow, would it?"

I couldn't meet her eyes.

Mom said Noah could leave his pajamas on inside out if he went straight to bed. Then she made us both a cup of herbal tea with honey, and we sat at the kitchen table.

"Tell me the whole story," Mom said.

So I did. I told her about Astrid and Nerf's perform-off in the school cafeteria and how Astrid texted me later to say the principal hadn't appreciated her *Hairspray* reference.

"I've always liked Astrid," Mom said.

I took a sip of warm, sweet tea and told Mom about Galit's three tips.

"Keep the confidence, lose the speed-talking," Mom said. "This is your d'var Torah, not a debate tournament."

"And then Dad made a spreadsheet. With eight columns and fourteen rows," I said. "Color coded."

"Oy." Mom's eyes rolled to the ceiling. I didn't know parents were capable of such epic eye rolls. Impressive.

Mom took a deep sip of tea. "I think I see the problem."

The problem was, I had gathered advice from the most important people in my life and I was more confused than ever.

"Dani, your d'var Torah isn't a big Broadway production, with singing, dancing, and comedians."

"No dinosaur fart jokes?"

"No. And no stage parents with complicated spreadsheets. Sometimes, Dani, it's you and only you in the spotlight."

"Like Pseudolus in *A Funny Thing Happened on the Way to the Forum*?"

"Except *you* don't have to be funny. You don't have to talk circles around the audience. You don't have to dance. You don't even have to sing." Mom looked at her spattered hands. "The only thing that *Forum* has in common with Va'era is that Pseudolus and Moses are both working toward freedom from slavery."

"More Moses, less Pseudolus," I said.

Mom reached out to stroke my hair. Her smile was tired but full of love.

"Go back to your Torah portion. You'll figure it out." Mom stood up. "I've got to wash this paint off."

I went upstairs. I fixed my pajamas. I sat on my bed and reread my parashah.

Mom was right; the answer had been there all along. Va'era isn't only about the Ten Plagues. It's also about Moses being reluctant to speak. He feels like no one ever listens to him. Not the Israelites, and definitely not Pharaoh. He tries to get out of it, telling the Lord, "I am of closed lips."

I, Dani Karet, could relate—at least a little bit.

A feeling of calm washed over me. Maybe it was the herbal tea, or maybe I finally realized that I could do this. I could talk about stepping up, especially when you think you can't, and leading your community. Even if it was only for three to five minutes.

I bounced off my bed and over to my desk, happy to see that Noah had put my pen back in its exact spot. He wasn't so bad, as brothers go.

I sat down, opened my notebook, and looked at my doodle of a tubby man in a toga.

"See you, Pseudolus."

I turned to a blank page.

I was ready to write. Words were coming to me, about to flow directly from brain to pen to paper.

I picked up my pen, pushed the button.

Water squirted down the front of my pajamas.

There was a giggle outside my door, then the sound of nine-year-old feet running from the scene of the crime.

The speech could wait another minute. Noah Karet was about to be in a pickle.

Glossary

Hebrew is used for Jewish prayer and study throughout the world and is the official language of Israel. Yiddish is a blend of Hebrew and German, developed by Eastern European Jews.

babka (Polish): sweet, braided bread

Bar/Bat Mitzvah (Hebrew): literally son/daughter of the commandment, but refers to both the person and the ceremony recognizing becoming an adult member of the Jewish community. The plural is B'nai Mitzvah.

bialy (Yiddish): small, round bread roll with a depression in the middle

bimah (Hebrew): podium

bubbe (Yiddish): grandmother

chochem (Yiddish): wise man

chub: foot-long ray-finned freshwater fish in the carp family often served in delis

chutzpah (Yiddish): brazenness

farbrecher (Yiddish): con man, crook

glick (Yiddish): good luck

haftarah (Hebrew): portion of the Book of the Prophets read after the Torah on the Sabbath

hamantashen (Yiddish): triangular cookies with sweet fillings often served at the Purim holiday

hora (Hebrew): circle group dance

Kadima (Hebrew): youth group affiliated with Conservative Judaism

kippah (Hebrew): flat, round head covering worn to express reverence for G-d; also yarmulke

klutz (Yiddish): clumsy or awkward person

kvetch (Yiddish): to complain

latke (Yiddish): fried potato pancake

madrich (Hebrew): youth group leader or teacher

mandelbrot (Yiddish): crunchy almond bread cookies

maven (Yiddish): expert

mazel tov (Yiddish): literally "good luck," but conveys congratulations

mensch (Yiddish): literally "man"; also a person of integrity and honor

meshuggener (Yiddish): foolish or crazy person

moreh (Hebrew): teacher

nosh (Yiddish): to eat a snack

parashah (Hebrew): section of the Torah to be read on the Sabbath

potschke (Yiddish): to fuss around inexpertly

rugelach (Yiddish): rolled crescent pastry with sweet filling

sable: two-foot-long North Pacific deep-sea fish with white flesh

schlemiel (Yiddish): incompetent person

schlimazel (Yiddish): unlucky or inept person

schmatta (Yiddish): rag; also ragged clothing

schmooze (Yiddish): talk or socialize

schmutz (Yiddish): dirt, grime, or rubbish

schnorrer (Yiddish): freeloader

shayna punim (Yiddish): pretty face

shpilkes (Yiddish): state of anxiety or impatience

shtetl (Yiddish): small Central or Eastern European town with a primarily Jewish population. Shtetls were wiped out by the Holocaust.

shul (Yiddish): synagogue

smelt: eight-inch-long silvery fish found in oceans, lakes, and rivers

spiel (Yiddish): long speech or sales pitch

sturgeon: very large, long-lived fish with cartilaginous skeletons

synagogue (ancient Greek): Jewish house of worship

tallit (Hebrew): prayer shawl worn by adults during certain Jewish religious services

tchatchke (Yiddish): knickknack

Torah (Hebrew): the Old Testament

tuchus (Yiddish): rear end, tush

tzedakah (Hebrew): right behavior as traditionally manifested among Jewish people by acts of charity

verklempt (Yiddish): overcome by emotion

zeyde (Yiddish): grandfather

Acknowledgments

Sarah Aronson: For my mom, for saving the pictures.

Nora Raleigh Baskin: To all the wonderful Jewish women role models, including Dr. Ruth, who once said, "A lesson taught with humor is a lesson retained."

Barbara Bottner: For my overdramatic, brave Polish Hungarian ancestors, with gratitude.

Stacia Deutsch: Thank you to the professors at Hebrew Union College-Jewish Institute of Religion who introduced me to Jewish writers of the past. And to Jonathan and Henry, who gave me this incredible opportunity to carry on the tradition.

Debbie Reed Fischer: Sincere thanks to Jonathan Rosen, Henry Herz, the Seymour Agency, and everyone at Albert Whitman & Company, as well as the people in real life who inspired characters in this semi-autobiographical story. Special gratitude goes to my husband, Eric, the love of my life, who supports me in every possible way. Lastly, a heartfelt thanks to my children, Louis and Sam, both of whom make me the proudest Jewish mother in the world.

Debra Green: Thank you to the wonderful PJ Library and its benefactors Harold Grinspoon and Diane Troderman.

Henry Herz: With thanks to the Author of all things; my parents for setting me on the path; my coeditor, Jonathan Rosen; and my gracious beta reader, Rabbi Alexis Berk.

Alan Katz: To Rabbi Jeremy Wiederhorn, who's always been there for us, on the bimah and off.

Nancy Krulik: For Ian, for reasons he knows only too well.

Stacie Ramey: Forever thanks to my parents who gave me the world. I'm going to keep it going for them as long as I can.

Jonathan Rosen: This anthology of Jewish stories has been a project close to my heart, and I'm extremely grateful to everyone who has had a hand in its making. My family for supporting me. Catriella Freedman from PJ Library, who was encouraging about the project. My agent, Nicole Resciniti, and Lynnette Novak, of the Seymour Agency for championing it. Andrea Hall from Albert Whitman, who believed in it and gave it a home. Henry Herz, who helped me bring it together and carry it across the finish line. To the amazing authors who jumped at the chance to participate and bring Jewish stories into the world. And finally, to all the kids who read it. I, sincerely, thank you all.

Melissa Roske: Gratitude to Jonathan Rosen for kicking off this amazing project and running with it; to Henry Herz for his hard work and dedication; and to the Seymour Agency, for brokering the deal. Thanks too to our eagle-eyed editor, Andrea Hall. And, as always, to my amazing family, Henry and Chloe. I love you to infinity and beyond.

Laura Shovan: I could not have written "A Funny Thing Happened on the Way to the Bimah" without the help of Meredith Lewis of PJ Library, Rabbi Tamara Miller, and Jaime Obletz. I thank them and authors Lenore Appelhans, Casey Lyall, and Michelle Rubin for their feedback.